I0684747

Death With Dessert

A Carol Sabala Mystery

Vinnie Hansen

Death With Dessert
A Carol Sabala Mystery

Copyright © 2015 Vinnie Hansen.

Published by: Misterio Press
www.misteriopress.com

Cover design: Book Cover Corner, www.bookcovercorner.com

Background cover painting: Daniel S. Friedman

ISBN-10: 0990874761

ISBN-13: 978-0-9908747-6-8

Hansen, Vinnie.

Death With Dessert / Vinnie Hansen — 2nd ed.

In memory of my father, Virgil W. Hansen

PRAISE FOR HANSEN'S WORK

Black Beans & Venom – Claymore Award Finalist and B.R.A.G. Medallion recipient.

"Her writing style is like liquid poetry. Her characters rule the page, and the action moves smoothly from one scene to the next."
Midwest Book Review

"I love Carol Sabala…quirky, gutsy and my kind of gal in an aqua tank top."
--Cara Black, Author of the Aimée Leduc mystery series

"With edgy precision, Hansen applies all the elements of a good mystery: interesting plot, compelling characters, a finely drawn sense of place, and excellent writing. One Tough Cookie *has made me a fan, one who can't wait to gorge on* Rotten Dates.*"*
--Denise Osborne, author of Feng Shui Mysteries and Queenie Davilov Mysteries

"Hansen's sense of humor and protagonist make for a good read. I particularly enjoyed her faithfully rendered Santa Cruz background."
--Laura Crum, author of the Gail McCarthy murder mystery series

"The pacing of Hansen's story is excellent."
--Chris Watson, *Santa Cruz Sentinel* on *Murder, Honey*

"I just finished Murder, Honey *and I found it splendid."*
--Laura Davis, author of *Courage to Heal*

"In Sabala, Hansen has created a likable sleuth whose many problems readers may readily identify with, and as far as Carol's mother goes—well, let's just say I hope we see more of her in the future."
--Michael Cornelius, *The Bloomsbury Review*

"Five silver pens out of five for 'Tang Is Not Juice.'*"*
--Silas Spaeth, *Salinas Californian*

"Best Book of Fiction of 2005" for Tang Is Not Juice
Oklahoma Writers' Federation, Inc.

ALSO BY VINNIE HANSEN:

Murder, Honey

One Tough Cookie

Rotten Dates

Tang Is Not Juice

Art, Wine & Bullets

Black Beans & Venom

Do not for ever with they vailed lids

Seek for they noble father in the dust

Thou know'st 'tis common; all that lives must die

Passing through nature to dust.

Shakespeare, *Hamlet*, Act I, Scene II

1999

CHAPTER 1

My mother's death precipitated the journey. Wind blew the rain sideways and buffeted my Karmann Ghia. The wild drops—warmer than the cold curved asphalt—sent up tendrils of steam like ghosts. My mother's death had launched this mission. My mother's death and a pink envelope.

My puny windshield wipers sluiced the blinding sheets of water. For once I was glad to have a back compartment loaded with junk, giving the car traction. The vehicle was also weighted down with a full tank of gas, and a single carry-on bag stuffed so full it felt like a load of bricks. Still I gripped the steering wheel with both hands, wishing there were taillights to follow, someone to run defense through the rocks washed onto the road. But it was seven a.m. on New Year's Day and I had Highway 17 to myself.

Willie Nelson's song "On the Road Again" played in my head, even though it didn't fit. I could count my trips for the last decade on one hand.

But now my mother's death had propelled me from Santa Cruz. She had died of the flu. It didn't seem right. In the year before her death, she had survived three surgeries—one to install a stent, another to remove a tumor in her stomach, and a third to transplant a pig's aortic valve into her heart.

When my mom woke from her third operation, she looked at me, smiled wanly, and oinked.

How could she have succumbed to the flu? She should have

died from something commensurate to my grief—burned at the stake, washed away in a tsunami, rotted by leprosy.

I merged onto the 85 Freeway. Mom's death had left me alone in the world. So what if I was over forty? I felt like an abandoned baby. Especially since my boyfriend and I had decided upon a hiatus. My brother Donald had died years ago. Only my father remained--maybe.

My little car glided like a kid on a Slip 'n Slide. I reduced my speed to a crawl and looked forward to the bumpy, chewed-up surface of 101.

My father, Geraldo Sabala, had deserted the family when I was a baby. At least that was the version I'd always been served. Now I doubted even those meager crumbs. Donald had not been able to remember our father, and Mom, a reticent person to begin with, developed lockjaw when it came to the topic of Geraldo Sabala. All she let escape was "that poor man" or "drunken fool."

She was harsher on herself. "It's not like I was a spring chicken," she'd say. "I wasn't exactly wet behind the ears. No sirree, I just thought I had to be like everyone else—get married and have kids."

Bit by painful bit, I'd extracted the frame of a story. She'd passed thirty and pounced on the first man who presented himself and seemed willing.

Now, armed with the only picture of my father I'd ever seen, I was off to track him down. I was, after all, a private investigator.

CHAPTER 2

Coyote Gee scanned the thirteen people. They sat silently in the dim cinderblock garage on old stained couches he had scrounged from here and there. His new clients included one family—father, mother, three kids. He did not worry about the teenaged girl. She had lived long enough to do hard work. The boy, about eleven, was wiry and athletic. But the little girl, maybe eight, made him fiddle with his bushy mustache.

The man should have left his family in their pueblo. Most of them did. It was the safest thing. Whether it was the right thing, he could not say. You could feel like a burro carrying the weight of regret.

He had been seeing more of this—men with families. The clampdown on the usual crossing spots pushed customers to him in the desert. The desert was not a place where men wanted to go back and forth, so they brought the whole family and stayed in the United States. So much for *La Migra*'s brilliant way to reduce illegal immigrants.

All thirteen customers regarded him warily. *Naturalmente.* The stories sprouted like cacti—coyotes who strapped people with fifty-pound bundles of food and water that turned out to be bricks of marijuana or cocaine. Try explaining that to *La Migra.*

There were the rides that didn't materialize. Safe houses that weren't safe. Coyotes who stole your money and deserted you.

"You are going to face two enemies," Coyote Gee said quietly in Spanish. Neither of them is me, he wanted to say. In spite of his graying hair and potbelly, he knew he appeared frightening with his strong arms and the scars on the right side of his face from trying to run up the freeway, against traffic, into the United States. A suicide mission. A method for young boys only.

The wife pressed close to her husband, the little girl backed in between her knees. She reminded Coyote Gee of his granddaughter, before she obtained eleven years and became an unfathomable creature. The women in this family all wore dresses.

"The first is *La Migra*," he said. "Do not let their faces or Spanish fool you. A lot of them over there are Mexican-Americans." He chuckled. "Maybe their padres came over with me."

They were all too dry-mouthed to smile. He knew how it felt. "Remember they are coconuts, brown on the outside, white in the center."

He wanted to pace, like a schoolmaster without a chalkboard, but he forced himself to stand still, to look calm. "If we encounter *La Migra*, we have two choices. We can stick together and they will round us all up and deport us. Or, we can grenade, split and run and try to confuse them." He usually opted for the latter. In his experience, *La Migra*—the Immigration and Naturalization Service that patrolled the borders—did not like to shoot people. Even coconuts do not want to injure someone from their father's pueblo.

Coyote Gee had already thought about ways to split them.

He had repeaters, one, Rogelio, who had been successful, twice, only to grow homesick and return to Mexico where he reacquainted himself with the skinny cows and lack of running water that had driven him north in the first place. He claimed to be Michoacano, but he had the kinky hair of a Salvadorian or Nicaraguan.

The other two repeaters were brothers who had been caught and deported together. The repeaters should be split up, the experience spread around, but it was hard to get family members to separate. He could see them, almost imperceptibly, huddling closer. He had one young couple. The man kept his arm around her shoulder, held her close. There was no one else to trust. You could not trust other people in the group. Even though they had been referred to him, you could not trust a coyote. And he could not trust them either.

If it worked out, another way to divide the group could be by destination. If they were from the highlands of Jalisco, they would be bound for Union City. If they were from the town of Aguililla, Michoacán, they would head for Redwood City. Tuxpeños would travel all the way to The Hamptons. Lots of Mexican cities had sister cities in the United States.

He would work out the groups later. "We are not going to cross here," he explained. He told them this so when they started off to the west, they would not think he was taking them to the desert to kill them. There were dirt roads that ran out along the fence, but any vehicle on those roads was immediately suspected. Coyote Gee preferred a circuitous, less-obvious route.

None of them wanted to cross from Naco, Mexico, to Naco, Arizona, anyway. Talk about two sister cities, these were Siamese twins, named with the last two letters of Arizona and the last two letters of Mexico. Some people said the letter thing was just a coincidence, that *naco* came from the Apache Indian word for the fruit of the barrel cactus. Others said the name had to do with the destination of a railroad line. These days *naco* meant about the same as hillbilly.

But Naco, Mexico, had been established first and was twelve times the size of Naco, Arizona, which seemed to exist only to house INS agents.

"Can any of the women drive?" he asked. Besides the family, the three repeaters, and the young couple, the group included three men, a young one, a middle-aged one and one that looked like he could be sixty.

The woman in the couple raised her hand. She was dressed in denim jeans, maybe a little too tight to be practical, a loose dark-colored blouse and sneakers. She had long hair, but she wore it in layered waves. Coyote Gee had imagined she might have city experience. This was lucky.

"You will drive," he said.

"Why?" her young man challenged.

She turned to her boyfriend. "*Esta bien, cariño*. I can do this."

Coyote Gee walked over to the family, squatted and introduced himself formally to the man, who was named Guadalupe Peralta. His wife, Maria, his oldest daughter Maria, his son Antonio, and his little girl Lupita.

Coyote Gee smiled slightly. He wanted to say that his wife had been named Maria, too. That he transported people for Maria. Instead, with old-fashioned, formal *cortesía*, Coyote Gee asked permission for Lupita to ride in the front with the young woman. They would be traveling in a minivan, he explained, with Arizona plates and he wanted the front to look like tourists. He kept the word *stupid* to himself.

The arrangement would be just a bit less suspicious than a Vanoline with a man at the wheel, he thought, but sometimes luck was found in bits.

He flashed a smile. It was a winning smile. Many women had told him so.

"*¿M'ija?*" the father asked tenderly of his daughter.

M'ija, M'ija, M'ija. Even after all these years, the word stabbed Coyote Gee's heart. Somewhere he had a daughter. His son had been given an American name, after his wife's father, and that was all well and good. But his little girl had been named Carolina, after his own mother, and Guadalupe, for the blessed virgin.

Now this girl backed into her mother's protection, but timidly nodded yes, she would do it, she would ride up front with a stranger.

This precaution of putting the women in front might prevent Coyote Gee from greasing a palm. The darkened windows would help to hide the others.

Coyote Gee had no use for cramming a person into the dash, suffocating people in a trunk, or burying people under a load of watermelons. Why use a checkpoint when there were close to two thousand miles of border, most of it wide open? The best way was not to be stopped or questioned in the first place, on either side of the border. They would be plenty crowded in the back of the minivan, but the desert night was cool, and the car had air-conditioning. Compared to the ways he had tried to cross, he thought, rubbing the scar on his cheek, his customers traveled first class.

"I also have other clothing for your women." Coyote Gee nodded to paper bags overflowing with discarded clothing. "They need to be dressed to run." They also needed to be dressed in dark clothing, but he didn't have to explain that. All the clothes in the bag were dark. He pointed to a corner of the room curtained with blankets. "They can change there."

He strode back to face the group. "The second enemy is more dangerous than *La Migra*. The second enemy could not care less if it kills you. The second enemy is the desert."

CHAPTER 3

The jet taxied to its runway. I imagined I could still yell, "Stop," jump off the plane, and sprint across the watery tarmac. Instead, I closed my eyes as the plane sped down the concrete and lurched into the air.

When I was young, my mother didn't have money to take us on many trips, but she did take Donald and me to meet our Grandma Turner. "I think you ought to meet your grandma before she kicks the bucket," was the romantic way my mom suggested the vacation.

I was ten and found everything about the drive from Ferndale to the San Francisco Airport exotic, from crossing the Golden Gate Bridge, to my mom's sweep through Haight Ashbury so Donald and I could see the hippies.

On the plane to Wisconsin, the stewardesses in their perfect make-up and crisp uniforms and the plastic trays of food with all the little packages enchanted me. I had fought Donald for a turn at the window seat.

The charm had faded long ago. I was now an aisle-seat passenger who packed plenty to read. I counted the rows to the exit, so I could find my way even if I were crawling through smoke. I wasn't ten anymore. Aging made a person cynical. Plus, in the last few years, I had been bashed on the head, shot at, and nearly strangled, which had accelerated the process.

But at this moment, I felt pretty good. Traveling on New Year's Day had provided not only a great airfare, but also an uncrowded plane. The middle seat was empty. A man occupied the window seat. So far, he'd been quiet, a good sign. He had the sturdy, conservative look of a military man, short cropped brown hair graying at the temples, muscles pressing at a short-sleeved tee shirt. Not a bad look. Actually, a pretty fine look. I liked strong jaws and noses that some might regard as too large. I pulled my gaze away.

Once we reached cruising altitude, I dug my fanny pack from under the seat and extracted a small packet left to me by my mother. She'd also left me what seemed a small fortune, making this trip possible. But the packet, carefully wrapped in a Ziploc bag, did not contain the records of her investments. I extracted a small rectangular photo with scalloped edges.

During youthful snooping, I discovered my mother's secret stash of chocolates and knew where she hid her diaphragm (not that I thought my mom had sex), but until her death, I had never seen this photo.

It was us, as a family.

The picture was in black and white. My mom wore dark baggy pants and a blouse with a Peter Pan collar. She had thick, wavy hair to her shoulders and looked shockingly like me. She gripped the hand of a little, already handsome, Donald.

Beside her stood the rakish devil, Geraldo Sabala. He was barely taller than my mom, but he had the same big smile that I'd seen throughout my youth on my brother's face. And there I was, swaddled, nestled against his chest. I imagined a manly scent brushed my nose and the flannel shirt comforted my cheek.

His proud smile cut into me now like razor blades. My sharp intake of air was almost a gasp. David Shapiro had a similar grin.

David and I were taking time apart to explore "other options." But if either of us acted on this arrangement, our relationship would be over. So the current situation was a celibate holding pattern, a bit like a stare down. Who would turn away first? My eyes flicked back to the man one seat away. He was absorbed in a paperback. No rings on his strong hands.

My mom had left me a note with the photo.

Dear Carol,

I thought you might like to have this. I don't know why I hung on to it. I wonder if I made the right decision in keeping your father out of your lives. Maybe if Donald had had a father, he would have turned out differently. I know people say they are born that way, but I've heard that gay men have overbearing mothers.

I'd read this letter many times, but I stopped again to marvel at my mom's use of the word "gay." Writing had forced her hand. What was she going to say, "men like that"? And even though she'd managed not to put the word in the same sentence with Donald, this was still her first public acknowledgment, at least to me, of his sexual orientation. My heart constricted at her silent guilt.

I was angry when your father left, because he left you kids. I didn't think he deserved to be part of your lives. I hope that you have forgiven me for this decision.

He did have good qualities. He was, as you can see, very handsome. He was also charming and clever. Even though he drank like a fish, he was a hard worker. And he loved you and Donald.

I didn't think I'd write that in a million years. How could someone who loves his children leave them? I never understood that one, so I've spent my life saying it wasn't true.

But I have memories that tell me differently. I see him with Donald on his shoulders. I hear him calling you M'ija.

To give the man a fair shake, life was hard for him in the United States, hard for all Mexicans. I should give him some credit, I suppose, for sticking around until you were born.

As I get older, Carol, I think maybe I made a mistake about how I raised you and Donald. That's why I'm leaving you this photo of your father.

This is for him. Love, Mom

She had enclosed a small pink envelope. Geraldo Sabala was printed on the front. Duct tape, the mark of my mom, sealed the back, but she had never used a pink envelope in her life.

CHAPTER 4

¡Hijole! The girl, Chabela, could drive, but she was not very good.

"There was a dead animal in the road," she said.

Coyote Gee bit his lip. He had had two wives. It was no use trying to explain to a woman that it was okay to run over small road kill, that it was safer than swerving. He drew a deep breath. Having the girl drive left him free to watch for the spot.

He loved the desert at night. Even crouched between the girls, with the odors of the eleven others rising toward him, their sweat, lingering tobacco, and acrid nervousness, he imagined the cool cleanness of the air. He could sense its stillness. The stars popped out brilliantly overhead, but there was no moon.

"Stop here."

Chabela did as he said, although there was nothing at the spot. She looked back to her husband Ricardo, lost in darkness. The couple reminded him of himself and his second wife Maria. They had met on a border crossing. He had been trying to get back to his family, but by then it had all seemed so hopeless, and Maria, well. . . .

Chabela's chest heaved. Who wouldn't be nervous? They all knew the stories of coyotes who turned out to be *banditos*, who pulled out *pistolas*, stole their stakes, and dumped the passengers in the middle of nowhere, a place like this.

Coyote Gee turned and gave the group another inspection. Everyone had water. Shiny canteens had been painted black. Each one had a black plastic garbage bag, something to sleep on if it came to that.

"I have to drive now," he told Chabela. They switched places inside the van. She would have liked to sit with Ricardo, but there was no space. He knew that feeling of aching to be close. To this day, he worked as a coyote for Maria. To stay connected. Because if Maria had been in the United States, maybe she would not have died.

Without turning on the headlights, Coyote Gee drove the minivan off the side of the road and headed across the desert. The more the INS clamped down on the easier crossing points, the more customers he had. The closer he could get them to Three Points, the better. The two advantages of crossing here: the space was wide open and the mesquite offered good coverage from aerial surveillance.

"¡*Chingale*!"

This was not a word you wanted to hear from your coyote. The men in the back rumbled.

"What's wrong?" Ricardo asked.

"They have repaired the fence," he said. He turned off the engine and climbed out of the van. He slid open the side door. "You two come with me." In the dark, he leaned in close to point at Ricardo and his experienced repeater. The repeater scratched at his arms like he was nervous, but that was normal. A border crossing could turn a macho man into a quivering Chihuahua.

Coyote Gee dragged a toolbox from the van along with his large Craftsman flashlight and its battery-pack stand. It provided just enough light to work by; automobile lights at the fence drew the INS like magnets. "We have to work fast," he whispered, "but quietly. Noise travels in the desert." He handed them wire cutters. "Big enough to drive through," he instructed. His job was to get them across this barren section.

Coyote Gee sighed at the endless cycle. They built fences and the Mexicans cut them, climbed over them, went around them, and dug under them, and so it would be until there were no more Mexicans who had eaten nothing but tortillas for a week.

Coyote Gee did a quick scan for any sky tower, the glassed boxes craned into the sky like robot aliens with metal legs. The INS used these portable observation posts along this stretch of the border.

He did not see one, but still, the newly repaired fence was bad news.

Very bad news.

Then he turned and saw the gun. Worse news still.

CHAPTER 5

This adventure could be a big mistake. I hoped, at least, that it would pry me out of my grief. It seemed better to stay active. At home, everywhere I turned, I ran into memories of my mother—all those irritating odd-colored throws and slippers she had knitted for me. The patchwork quilt I pulled up to my neck each night no longer comforted me. On the quilt my mom had said to hell with using whatever was at hand and had selected colors I would like: deep forest green and dusty rose with a little gold for sparkle, and an earthy brown. The whole thing was heavy, and durable, with a soft flannel backing. I couldn't pack away the blanket, but I was exhausted by the thoughts it stirred and by the endless psychoanalysis of how my mother had sewn a statement of our relationship—a crazy quilt.

After the funeral, after bouts of tears, I'd driven to Eureka, to the County Recorder's Office. I had filled out a form, paid a fee, and received the marriage record for Geraldo Sabala and Bea Turner. It had been that easy.

In the musty room I stared at the document. My father was born in Zihuatanejo, Guerrero, Mexico, on October 13, 1928.

October 13th was David's birthday! Logically, with only three hundred and sixty-five days in a year and approximately six billion people on earth, a shared birthday did not even rank as a coincidence.

But logic did nothing to dispel the heebie-jeebies. After seeing the photo of my father, with his short stature and blazing smile, I wondered if my subconscious had picked a man like him, even if I had no memory of him.

The trip to Eureka had been all business. I didn't take any detour to my hometown of Ferndale. It may have been a quaint village to tourists, but to me it represented one square mile of boredom. Tourists adored the peaceful downtown and the Victorian houses; they probably dreamed of how idyllic it would be to live there. But to a teenager, Ferndale was Hell. We had made our fun, drinking beer and skinny-dipping in the Eel River. I still stayed in touch with a couple of high school friends in Ferndale. But I was on a quest and there had been no time for a walk down memory lane.

"Excuse me."

I startled. The man at the window seat wanted to get up.

"Long legs," he said in way of apology.

I backed into the narrow passageway. "I understand," I said. "That's why I like the aisle. I can stretch my legs."

"Smart," he said.

I glowed. I loved being called smart.

The man stood right in front of me and stretched, pulling the steel blue tee from his khakis and revealing a sliver of hard stomach.

I remained standing, uncertain when the man planned to return to his seat.

"I'm going to walk up and down," he announced.

"Good idea," I said. "Blood clots can be deadly."

His eyes took me in. Their color matched his tee shirt exactly. Other than that, I couldn't tell a thing. I couldn't tell if he thought my comment wise, or the stupidest remark he'd heard in his life.

Flushing, I sat in my seat. The blush turned into fire and perspiration dampened my forehead. I reached up to open the air vent. These hot flashes had been happening to me with increasing regularity, but when I told my doctor, she stated unequivocally, "You are too young to be menopausal."

The man walked to the curtain that divided coach and first class. He raised his right arm, bent it at the elbow. He lifted his other arm and used its hand to push on the elbow, edging the right hand down his back. His bicep bulged into a boulder. I glanced across the aisle and realized I wasn't the only woman fixated on the spectacle.

I forced my thoughts back to my trip to Eureka. The stop at Uncle Teddy's in Garberville. That had been enlightening.

Teddy was my mother's much younger brother, a late life surprise for my grandparents. I despised the man.

He lived in a sunny ranch-style house with a well-tended front lawn and rows of fussily maintained rose bushes along the front. His wife Doreen was always quick to point out all the things Teddy did around the house.

When I rang the bell, I expected Teddy to answer. He worked at home now, like the spider he was, doing Web design.

The young man who opened the door took my breath away. "Brandon!" I'd forgotten about winter break.

"Hey, Carol." My one and only cousin gave me a rib-crushing hug. If Brandon had only come without parents. . . .

He released me. I drew a breath and grinned. "Are you ready to graduate?"

He smiled shyly. "I guess so." He was tall and slender like his father, but more buffed. His porcelain skin, light brown hair and hazel green eyes came from his mother, but Brandon infused the features with personality. I'd seen him not long ago at my mother's funeral, but I was still stunned that this hand-some man had evolved from my little freckle-faced cousin.

I asked him about colleges.

"I actually applied to UCSC."

"You actually did," I teased him. "That's great. Santa Cruz is wonderful. You'll be able to surf." The idea that Brandon might wind up in my town buoyed me. "Have you visited the campus?"

He glanced away, down the hall for his dad. This told me that they had. I tried to shake off the hurt. After all, on a normal occasion, I would have continued straight through Garberville. I wouldn't have stopped to visit them, either.

Uncle Teddy appeared from the hallway. He had managed to become sixty without ever having had a real occupation. Both Teddy and his son Brandon had been late-life surprises to their mothers.

"Well, hello there," Uncle Teddy said to me. "Has something come up with the estate?"

"You could say that."

Teddy had felt entitled to be my mom's executor and hadn't forgiven me for receiving the position. My mom never stopped taking care of me, as much as I might have believed the reverse were true this past year. She'd sold our family home in Ferndale when she'd retired to Santa Cruz, and invested the money wisely. She'd been able to pay for her residential care and still leave me a tidy sum. To Brandon she left money in trust for college tuition. To Teddy she left one dollar and some memorabilia. As executor, I had one final task—to deliver a pink envelope. I held on to that as the rational underpinning for my trip to Mexico.

"I've gotta jam," Brandon said, taking an oversized gray-hooded sweatshirt from the hall closet and pulling it over his head. "It was great seeing you, Carol."

Teddy didn't invite me to the kitchen for coffee, but instead beckoned me to follow him. Even though Teddy wore belted slacks and a dress shirt with a tee underneath, he padded down the hallway in his stocking feet.

He plopped into a comfy computer chair.

I took the nearby straight-backed chair, set up for clients, I guessed.

He swiveled toward me. "So what do you want?"

Whew, I thought. When my mother was alive, Teddy had tried a lot harder to be nice. Death had washed away the saccharine coat and left raw hostility.

"I want to ask you some questions about my dad."

CHAPTER 6

The guy Coyote Gee had chosen to help with the fence was not very big. But he pointed the pistol like he meant business. He remained outside the arc of the flashlight and jittered as he commanded them to throw down their tools. He jabbed the weapon in and out of the light.

The gun was a nine millimeter semi-automatic. Coyote Gee complied with the young man's wishes and cursed himself. He had a revolver for such occasions, but it was in the van with all his helpless customers. Many of them would be carrying cash, start-up money for the United States. These people in the United States who said, "Send 'em back," didn't realize there was nothing to go back to. Many had sold everything they had to pay him. Coyote Gee's heart sank like lead.

He felt stupid. Caught flat-footed. This was the natural time to do the crime, when they were occupied with a problem and south of the border. If you were heading north, it was better to leave any bodies in Mexico. Not that it mattered much when you crossed over into Pima County. They had John Does stacked up in freezers.

The young man swung the gun first at Ricardo and then at him. "Give me your money," he said in Spanish.

Coyote Gee forced a laugh. "I don't bring no money. Do I look like a fool?"

"What's going on?" Chabela called out the open side door.

"Stay inside, *mensa*," the robber said.

"Is this a stick-up?" Chabela cried hysterically. "Please, please, please, I beg on my knees, before the Blessed Virgin I plead, do not shoot him!"

In spite of himself, Coyote Gee's attention whirled toward

the van. He had to agree with the robber. Chabela was acting like a fool. He never would have guessed she would be the one to lose her head. There was not a peep from the children. Not a word from their mother. But then, who could hear anything over Chabela's racket?

The robber pointed the pistol at the van and growled for her to shut her mouth.

"¡*Mi amor*!" Chabela wailed.

Coyote Gee observed that Chabela did not seem to care one *frijolito* about him.

The robber turned the gun back to Ricardo.

Chabela screeched like a bad actress on a *telenovela*.

Ricardo slowly bent down. "My money is in my sock," he explained to the robber.

"Tell your woman to shut her fucking mouth," the young man barked.

Ricardo glared up at him and slowly extracted a roll of bills, but he did not call out to Chabela. Instead he extended the money halfway to the man and began to talk to him softly and earnestly in Spanish. "So you are in such a hurry to be a *gringito* that you will rob the people of your blood?"

"Don't talk to him!" Chabela shrieked. "He will kill you."

As the robber leaned down for the money, a figure rushed from behind the van. He grabbed the young man's hair, snapped back his head, and pressed a knife to his throat.

The blade glinted. "I have slit the throats of many pigs," the man hissed.

The thief dropped the money and the gun.

Everything made sense now to Coyote Gee. The ruse of Chabela's screaming so the man could crawl out the driver's-side door without being detected.

Coyote Gee made out the shadowy form. The father. Of course. Protecting his family, the way any father should do.

CHAPTER 7

My row mate had finished his display of toe touches and knee bends and isometrics that showed off his triceps and the full wedge of his torso.

I stood to let him back into his seat.

"Thanks." He picked up his paperback.

Normally I was thankful to have a quiet reader for a neighbor, but the man's lack of interest piqued me. He wasn't traveling with a woman. He had no gay vibe. He didn't wear a wedding ring. I pulled my wild auburn hair over my shoulder.

He turned the cover of his paperback toward me. "*A Simple Plan*," he said. "Good book."

Heat crept up my body. He must have seen me checking out his hand. In a moment, I was going to perspire like a petty thief in court. I smiled, unbuckled, and headed for the restroom at the back of the plane.

When I returned, the woman across the aisle had moved into my seat. She was blonde, perfectly tanned, and younger than I was. She was chatting with Mr. Muscles and didn't glance up at my presence. I admired her quickness and boldness.

Mr. Muscles cleared his throat.

She made no move to get out of my seat, perhaps hoping that I'd volunteer to sit elsewhere so as not to interrupt her in-progress seduction. When no such offer escaped my lips, she asked in a perky voice, "This seat is open, isn't it?"

Before either of us could respond, she scooted her size-three body into the middle seat and proceeded to yak. To escape, I moved across the aisle to her seat and stuck my nose into my own paperback.

From the air, Zihuatanejo looked like Santa Cruz, curving around a bay. According to my Internet info, the bay had been considered insignificant by the Spanish explorers and so Zihuatanejo had remained an undisturbed fishing village. It still lacked high rises, and mountainous jungle forced the town to nestle the water.

The plane touched down smoothly. I popped from my seat, muscled my one bag from the overhead bin, and disembarked behind a few passengers from first class. I followed them across the tarmac toward the single terminal building. The humidity plastered my long sleeved shirt to my skin and turned my Levi's into instruments of bondage. I felt like a steaming cauliflower. I swiped my shirtsleeve across my dripping forehead.

In mid-wipe, I heard, "Zihuatanejo is the getaway in *The Shawshank Redemption.*" My handsome seatmate appeared beside me. He shouldered a black overnight bag and pulled a small suitcase on wheels.

"Huh?" I asked eloquently, caught off-guard by the Now-I-Can-Talk Phenomenon. People who traveled with you for five hours, with little more than an "excuse me," would, upon touchdown, pour out their life stories, secure in the knowledge that should you be a horrendous bore with halitosis, or in my case, an overcooked, stinky vegetable, at least they wouldn't be stuck with you for more than a few minutes.

"*The Shawshank Redemption,*" he prompted.

"Oh, yeah, the movie. I didn't see it."

I looked back to see what had become of Blondie.

He followed my gaze. "Are you traveling with someone?"

We entered the terminal and took our spots in the roped off labyrinth leading to four passport windows.

"No."

"Are you going to Zihua?"

I nodded and tried to disguise my sweat swipes as merely pushing back my hair. With an attempt at air-conditioning, the small terminal building provided relief. The floor looked like it could be real marble tile, and blue pillars and fuchsia walls announced we were in the tropics. The official stamped our passports and we entered a room with one baggage carousel.

"Would you like to share a cab into town?"

I looked up at him. He didn't smile and the gray-blue eyes were unreadable. My face, I've frequently been told, is like an open book, and he apparently read my doubt.

"The cabs have a fixed fare whether there's one passenger or four, so why not save ten bucks?"

"Sure," I said.

"Is that all your luggage?"

"I'm a light traveler."

"Good," he said. "Me, too." He stepped confidently up to a post with a button on it. He pressed it and a stoplight lit up with a green *PASE*. I started to walk with him toward the glass doors, but a uniformed woman indicated that I needed to press the button, too.

I backed up and luckily received a green light.

In the lobby a circle of Mexican men greeted us.

"Where you go?"

"You need taxi?"

I followed my new friend to a window. "Taxi. Zihua. Two." He laid down a crisp twenty and stared at the teller on the other side of the glass. His eyes and the money communicated perfectly. He didn't engage in any of the overly friendly, badly spoken Spanish of the usual tourist. The man was a little scary, and I liked it.

"Excuse me a minute." I crossed to a public phone and scanned the phone book for a listing for Geraldo Sabala. If he lived here, if he had a phone, it was unlisted. The entire weight of my unrealistic expectation landed. As much as I tried to tell myself I was coming to Zihuatanejo because I deserved a vacation and I could now afford one, that I was just going to check around for my dad to see if I could deliver the pink envelope, the truth was I expected him to be here for me, as surely as if he were waiting for my plane.

But there was no proof he'd even returned to Mexico, much less to this place of his birth. An Internet search of his name had revealed nothing usable.

My acquaintance and I walked back into the heat to a line of white taxis. A manager type took our slip of paper and directed us to a car.

"Zihua. Hotel de los Milagros Grandes," my acquaintance told the driver. "Where are you going?" he asked me. He extracted Bucci sunglasses from his suitcase and slipped them on.

My last couple of years with David had sharpened my sensitivity to forces ready to commandeer my life. They stirred a panicky need to assert myself.

"*Por favor*, a Hotel Villas Rosa en Playa Ropa," I said. "*Atrás de* Villa Mejicana."

Mr. Muscles arched an eyebrow at me and smiled in amusement, rather than exhibiting the emotions I would have preferred—abashed, astonished, or better yet, impressed.

The driver wanted to load our bags in the trunk, but we both declined the offer.

As soon as we were situated in the back seat of the taxi, I handed Mr. Muscles ten dollars for my share of the cab fare. We rode in silence for a while through expanses of coconut palms. The vehicle was blissfully air-conditioned. Furry red dice danced below the rearview mirror.

"Nice," he said, relaxing into the seat. "In addition to everything else, you aren't a blabbermouth."

I smiled, happy to know the woman on the plane must have been torture for him. "In addition to what else?" I shamelessly fished.

"Good looks. Good Spanish. One bag."

I was so unprepared for this--the idea of being over forty and flirting. Before I had met David Shapiro, it had taken months for a friend to convince me to place a personal ad. No sooner did I place one than a woman met her killer through the ads. Entering the playing field seemed like tiptoeing through landmines.

Behind the dark glasses Mr. Muscles seemed to study the road ahead. He had delivered his flirtations as dryly as a to-do list.

"*Gracias*," I said. What a better word than thanks. It bestowed on the other person grace and blessings. If my father had stayed in my life, I wondered, would I be fluently bilingual?

I dug around in my pack to find my own sunglasses, tortoise shell plastic from Long's Drugs. A cheap retro look. I had a habit of losing sunglasses and couldn't afford to pay more than fifteen dollars a pair. Well, maybe now, with my mother's money, I could. I eyed Mr. Muscle's stylish Bucci's.

How often did I meet someone single, age-appropriate, physically appealing, and apparently interested? The encounter demanded some sort of decision about David. A finger found its way to my teeth, but I pulled it away before I bit the cuticle.

I leaned toward the driver and asked in Spanish, "How much time does it take to reach the hotel?"

"*Veinte minutos.*"

I had twenty minutes to make up my mind if I wanted to pursue this man or not. My stomach roiled with nervousness.

The taxi entered Zihuatanejo from the inland side of town. Small, unpainted concrete and block houses ran along the dry hillsides. Many had tin roofs. Bright blue, lemon yellow, pale pink, chalk orange or lime green—not colors Americans normally used on their houses—dotted the bleak landscape. I liked the way people in the tropics applied color. Of course, maybe the palette resulted from leftovers and rejects, the same way one might see a third-world kid running around in a Joe Camel tee shirt.

I couldn't keep gazing out the window without seeming a little rude. I didn't know what to do so I pulled myself back toward the driver and asked if he knew anyone in town named Geraldo Sabala. Sabala with an "s."

"*Sí.*"

"*Sí?*" I lurched forward and stared at the side of the man's face, middle-aged, chubby, and mustached. A sober family man, not a hint of a joker about him.

"*Vende* pizzas," the driver remarked.

"He sells pizzas!" I used the passenger seat to lever myself forward. This had to be some sort of joke.

The driver gave me a tolerant, crazy-tourist smile. "Very good pizza."

"You speak English?"

"Little," he said. "You like some pizza?" He flashed another nervous smile. "Cheaper than Round Table."

"Yes," I said, sinking back to my seat. "Forget the hotel. Take me to the pizza."

The cabbie turned to my companion.

My cab mate nodded. "Downtown first, then my hotel." He swiveled toward me. "I'm impressed. You found your man just like that." He snapped his fingers.

"Who says I was looking for a man?"

Mr. Muscles smiled thinly, which for him, seemed like the equivalent of a laugh. "The photo on the plane. Phone book check. The reaction just now. Pretty obvious, don't you think?"

Not to everyone, I thought. "What's your name?" My first impression of him had been military. Certainly he was observant. Maybe he was a cop.

"Mark Escalante." He held out his hand.

"Carol Sabala."

We shook, both with firm, business-like grips, as though trying to out-do one another in no-nonsense attitude. I reassured myself that getting to know this man did not violate my standing with David. Right now I had no standing with David. At this very moment, he could be chatting up a thirty-something in Trader Joe's.

The taxi entered the city proper, a concrete canal to the left, and the large Commercial Mejicana grocery store to our right. At the corner of its parking lot loomed a green plastic Christmas tree as tall as the store itself and decorated with giant red Coca-Cola bottle caps.

"So you're looking for a relative."

I shrugged. In spite of the air conditioning, my skin was starting to prickle, presaging another hot flash. I lifted my long hair, pulled it into a thick tail and started to twist it. Only now that I held a fistful of hair, did I cast around for an object that I could use to clip it.

"Dead-beat dad?" he ventured.

I scowled. I supposed it was a logical conclusion: the shared name, the old, black and white photo.

Mark reached into the side pocket of his carry-on and handed me a pencil. "Will this help?"

Yellow was not my color, but I accepted the classic number two and stuck it through my coil of hair. This man was positively unnerving.

"My former wife had the same kind of hair," he explained.

A chink in the armor? Was he signaling availability?

"Playa la Ropa to the left," the taxi driver said. "You still want pizza?"

"Yes."

Adrenaline churned in my stomach and zapped out to my nerve endings. What if it were this simple? What if in ten minutes I was meeting my father? Adrenaline rushes had always made me warm, but nowadays my body had no temperature gauge. A little squirt of adrenaline or a little flush of embarrassment and the next thing I knew I was in some sort of sweatbox torture hell.

Mark handed me a sock.

I looked dubiously at the white cotton. He seemed to have pulled it from behind his ear.

"It's clean." He nodded encouragingly. I patted.

We turned onto the town's main street, which demanded quality backseat driving. I mimed mine, clutching the back of the seat and planting my right foot. The driver ignored my brakes and shot into the next lane in front of another white taxi and behind a bus spewing diesel. He whipped to the left and I saw death barreling toward me in a black SUV.

CHAPTER 8

The wide-eyed tourist slammed on his brakes. A Mexican woman yanked her young daughter back to the curb out of our path. Our driver zoomed a hundred feet over bumpy cobblestone and screeched to a halt in bumper-to-bumper traffic. The red dice jumped. I rocked forward and then back into the seat. The driver emitted a common Spanish curse.

"How far is the pizza place from here?" I asked.

In Spanish he explained I should go to my left and walk a few blocks until I reached Paseo del Pescador along the Playa Principal, the main beach, and then ask anyone for La Pizza.

I climbed from the car and hoisted my bag to my shoulder with a grunt. Mark hopped out, too, and pulled the handle from his rolling suitcase. I raised my eyebrows in question.

"As long as we're stalled here, I may as well change my money. Plus, I'm hungry."

An awkward moment passed in which I was probably supposed to invite him along to La Pizza. But there were too many forces in opposition—David Shapiro back home, my reason for going to La Pizza, and my whole grubby existence. I tried to hand him his athletic sock.

"Keep it," he said.

I couldn't tell whether he was kind or disgusted.

"There's nothing sadder than a stray sock," I said.

"We'll pair them up later." He tossed the wardrobe bag over his shoulder and strode off toward the main drag.

He seemed mighty cocky and sure of himself, but that kind of guy had drawn me since my first dope-smoking, motorcycle-riding teenaged boyfriend. Nice, normal guys failed to stir my blood.

While all the taxis attested to a lively tourist industry, this was a real town, not a manufactured tourist destination, and Mexicans threaded along the narrow sidewalks. White faces pocked the crowds. I'd read in my tourist information that in 1968 the government had tried to develop the town, but the citizens had refused the idea of having tall buildings that blocked views of the bay. They didn't need no stinking resort. People who wanted a resort could go to nearby Ixtapa. The name meant "the white place," supposedly for the white sands.

I jolted with a sudden step down. There was no warning, no reason. The sidewalk simply dropped off. I collected my dignity. Welcome to the tropics.

I turned to the left at a bar, nothing more than a roll-up front with a single counter lined with stools. The whole thing could fit inside my kitchen. The men openly stared at me, the strange woman beating her left hand with a sock.

As I walked toward the beach, the shops became less utilitarian, the interiors more brightly lit and full of finely embroidered "traditional" white Mexican garb and silver jewelry crafted by local artisans. Some of the shops were closed in honor of the holiday.

My heart danced its own little salsa. Either the cabbie was mistaken about the name or this had to be an incredible coincidence. Surely my father had not deserted my mother, brother and me only to open a pizza parlor!

Tidbits of the conversation with my uncle Teddy floated through my head. He'd been a teenager when my father left. He didn't have much insight into his older sister's marriage.

"I do know things were hot for Mexicans," he said. "The government had this program called Operation Wetback."

The name squeezed my stomach. Leaning back in his computer chair and cracking his neck, Teddy issued the words calmly. "Can you believe they actually used that phrase?"

For no rational reason, I suspected he relished the words.

"What was Operation Wetback?"

Teddy stared at the ceiling, remembering. "You know how it is. People get a bee in their bonnet and start crying out against illegal immigration. Of course, they obviously don't mean just any immigrants. They mean Mexicans."

"So they souped up the border patrol?"

"Oh, it went way beyond that." Teddy flapped a slender hand. "The government actually organized state and local officials and invaded Mexican-American neighborhoods. I remember Bea and your dad were pretty worried."

"Do you think that's why my dad left?"

"It could be. They rounded up or scared away a lot of people."

I was astounded. I'd never heard of this. "All illegal?"

Teddy had shrugged.

Now I followed a jog in the road to reach the esplanade along the bay. Zihuatanejo had so much in common with Santa Cruz. It was a fishing town like Santa Cruz. It had a walkway along its Playa Principal, which translated to Main Beach, exactly what we called the central beach in Santa Cruz. In both towns the area was geared toward fish restaurants and tourists.

The town square was on the beach walkway. At its edge, I found a spot of shade under a tree, rested my heavy bag, and stopped to collect myself. In spite of the heat, boys played basketball in a sunken court and young folks lounged on the concrete tiers of steps to watch. The tiers and the retaining wall in front of the beach were painted ochre with terra cotta trim. Beyond the wall, the bay lapped the sand, calm and inviting. I approached a small cluster of teenagers and asked in Spanish for La Pizza.

A girl sucking a tamarindo lollipop pointed. "*Allá.*"

Sure enough, when I squinted, I could see the sign. I thanked her. I sat back down in the shade and mopped my face with Mark's sock. My heart pounded like the bass in gangster rap. The beat thrummed in my head.

I didn't consider myself a vain person, but I longed for a mirror. I imagined myself looking slightly crazed, my hair springing loose from an improvised bun stuck through with a pencil, my face sweaty, my mascara smeared, my clothes damp and smelly.

I lifted my pack and trudged toward La Pizza. My head spun. I forced myself to breathe slowly in and out.

La Pizza was a tiny place, with a few tables on the sidewalk, and a couple of tables inside. I took a table under the awning. I looked around to get my bearings. Only two tables were occupied, a young, shirtless man drinking a Corona and an American-looking couple with all the accouterments of tourists—Hawaiian shirts, money belts, Teva sandals, sunglasses, and baseball hats—making short work of a delicious-looking pepperoni pizza.

I peered through the dusty window. And there, right behind the counter, was my brother Donald.

CHAPTER 9

A skinny, long-haired girl who appeared all of thirteen meandered over to hand me a menu. I pointed to the man behind the counter and asked his name.

"¿*Mi papi?*"

I nodded.

She squinted at me, gathering thick lashes, and placed her pink flip-flop on top of her other foot. She wore a yellow apron over a sundress and was all bony arms and legs.

I explained that her father resembled my brother.

She smiled, but then took a disbelieving look at my fair complexion and "colored" eyes, as my Mexican-American friends called them. "Geraldo Sabala," she said, apparently concluding I was a harmless *tourista*.

I showed her my American money.

"It's okay," she said in English.

I ordered a beer. Clearly the man was not my father. And Donald, my brother, was dead. Before his cremation, I had attended the service, seen him emaciated and unreal in the satin lining of the coffin, heard the words Donald had chosen from Lewis Thomas' *The Lives of a Cell*. The man chopping something behind the counter was not Donald, but he looked the way Donald had before he became sick. He looked the way I liked to remember my brother.

The girl emerged from the kitchen with a tray bearing a frosted glass, a small plate of lime wedges, and a bottle of Modela Negro.

She asked if I would like to order some food. I shook my

head and pressed the cold beer to my cheeks before slugging down half the bottle. I used the mug to cool the back of my neck.

The man shoveled a pizza from the oven. His body rocked with the motion of cutting the crust. He was meatier than Donald had been, even before his illness, and he sported a mustache. But who knew what my brother might have looked like if he'd been healthy and lived another nine years. Maybe he would have gained a manlier heft. And he had, in his early twenties, experimented with a mustache. The man wiped his hands on his full-length apron and put the pizza on the counter. "*M'ija*," he called to his daughter.

The word slammed around in my brain like a hard-hit racquetball—*M'ija, M'ija, M'ija.* I put down my head, closed my eyes, steepled my fingers and pressed them, hard, to my lips. *M'ija* was a contraction of *mi hija*, my daughter. According to my mother, my father had called me that. *M'ija.*

I plucked myself from the swamp of sentimentality. Every Mexican father called his daughter that. When I'd investigated a case at a school, one teacher had told me of a girl who'd entered first grade thinking her name was *M'ija.*

The girl trotted by and delivered the pizza to the shirtless man.

I bit a lime to revive myself. I removed my sunglasses, marched to the counter and introduced myself in Spanish. When I said "Sabala," the man brightened. I asked if I could please talk to him for a moment.

"*M'ija*," he snapped. "Something wrong with your beer?" he asked me in English, with the impatience of an American.

"No, no, no. And your daughter's service was fine. I'd just like to talk to you for a minute."

He glanced around the tiny kitchen behind him. La Pizza was not busy, but on the other hand, he didn't seem to have any help besides his daughter. With my years of experience in a restaurant, I knew all the invisible work to be done—the slicing, dicing, chopping, replenishing, cleaning, bookkeeping. Most people who dreamed of owning their own little café had absolutely no idea what a consuming proposition it was.

"Zavala, huh? You don't look Mexican," he said as he hung up his tomato-paste-splotched apron. He commanded his daughter to finish washing the dishes, lifted the hinged door in the counter and came out to face me. He was about five ten, a little taller than I was, and shorter than Donald had been. He wore a blue knit shirt and brown polyester pants, but he showed no sign of being hot.

We shook hands. "You speak great English."

"My father spoke English," he explained. "He started teaching me since I was a kid."

I sat weakly on my chair. *Spoke.* I gestured for him to join me. "Was your father named Geraldo Sabala, too?"

His dark eyes widened. "Yes. Do you know him?" he asked eagerly.

Either this Geraldo Sabala had not mastered verb tenses, or he wasn't sure whether or not his father occupied the present. I shook my head. His dark eyes dimmed. "¡*M'ija*!"

I turned to see why he'd called his daughter.

Mark Escalante had stopped on the walkway to read the posted menu. He nodded to me. Was he following me, spying on this private moment? He may have been gorgeous, and I may have been a tinge flattered, but the red-haired part of me felt like sailing over the tables and throttling his neck.

"Excuse me," Geraldo Sabala said. He returned to his cell and strapped on his apron. The customer comes first, the golden rule of successful business, at least before the era of mega-corporations.

Mark strolled on. I glared at the back of the black wardrobe bag slung over his shoulder. I glanced back to Geraldo, but before he could untie his apron, a young couple plopped into the other table under the awning.

Fortunately, even if the mega-corporations made their way to Zihuatanejo, they could never stop some people from wanting the personal touch of a fresh-made pizza. If tourists flocked to Zihua to escape Starbuck's and WalMart, once the place was thoroughly Starfucked, *adios, amigos.* The tourists would move on to the next untainted, still charming place, leaving the boarded-up Carlos and Charley's in their wake.

Geraldo gave me a palms-up shrug. I strolled to the counter. "I would like to continue our conversation. Is there another time when I could talk to you?"

"What are we talking about?" His impatience had returned with donning the apron.

I realized his English, while smooth and only slightly accented, was not perfect. "Your father," I said, uncertainly.

"Why?"

His daughter trotted to the counter, rattled off an order, and then ducked under, slipped behind her father, and disappeared into the back room.

"I think he was my father, too."

"*Loca.*" Geraldo glowered and shooed me away with the back of his hand. "Go," he said roughly.

He started to lift the hinged part of the counter, but I backed toward the door with my hands up.

As I nearly stumbled over the threshold, his expression softened to bafflement. I was, after all, a woman. And a *gringa.* Confusion had been added to the menu.

CHAPTER 10

The airplane "snack" had consisted of two hard chocolate wafers. I was starving, but wired with excitement. My seemingly newfound half-brother turned away from me. I wanted to bound over the counter, grab him by the shoulders, shake him, and force him to talk to me. But he'd just picked up his chopping knife.

As I stood outside La Pizza, hitching up my pack after my clumsy exit, he shot me a warning glare that made me aware of my outsider status. This was his restaurant, his town, his country. I may have been a novice P.I., but I had learned a couple of things. Unless a person was completely hostile, in which case it didn't matter if you got up in his face, generally there was nothing to be gained by pissing him off.

I had to tamp down my excitement. I would give Geraldo some time to calm down, to mull over the idea we were related, and to grow curious. I had a week here and I'd already made amazing progress.

I edged out of the tiny sidewalk eating area and walked along the promenade where trinket booths and restaurants spread onto the beach. Beyond them fishing boats rocked in the gentle waves. Evening didn't promise to be any cooler. I had to get out of my Levi's, but this was not an easy proposition. Waiters and *maitre d's* trolled the walkway, watching for the early dinner crowd.

Making a sudden hard left, I marched directly to the back of a nice-looking fish restaurant. I was in the small restroom with the door locked before anyone could say, "Tilapia."

I exited in shorts and flip-flops feeling smug and much cooler. My sneakers beat jauntily against my pack as I bopped toward the sidewalk.

"Nice maneuver."

I wheeled, expecting to confront a manager.

Instead, Mark Escalante smiled up at me from one of the wicker chairs.

I froze in a moment of paranoid fantasy. Had David Shapiro hired this man to follow me?

Using his foot, Mark pushed out a chair at his table. "Join me."

"I haven't changed any money yet."

"It's New Year's. The banks are closed."

I would have felt embarrassed except I knew that he had forgotten, too.

"Dollars work fine," he said. "I am not stalking you," he added. "Sorry about what happened back there."

I wanted to swim in the ice of his margarita, splash in the clear greenness, and lick the salt from the rim of his glass. The drink looked mighty good. And so did Mark Escalante. Did the man ever sweat?

I sat. I leaned my bag against the chair holding his luggage. "What *happened back there?*"

In the restroom, I'd taken the opportunity to wipe off my face and put on some lipgloss, so as long as I kept on my sunglasses to hide the bags under my eyes, I looked okay. The waiter swooped by with a menu, and I ordered a margarita.

"You found your lead and I blew it."

His voice didn't waver. He had no doubt about his read of the situation.

I felt like singing out, "I may have located a half-brother," but I had a superstitious streak that believed good luck could be jinxed by talking about it. And it was more than that. Mark Escalante was not the right person for intimate sharing.

"So what were you doing there?" I asked.

"Searching for something to eat. I was reading the sign before I noticed where I was." He sipped his margarita and then studied it. "At these tourist restaurants at least we can be sure they use purified water for the ice."

I eyed his plate of food and asked him what he'd ordered.

"Snapper. I saw a man delivering the fish to the back door."

It was quite possible with the fishing boats in the harbor, and the name of the esplanade, Paseo del Pescador, Boulevard of the Fisherman.

When the waiter returned with my margarita, I ordered snapper Veracruzana.

The drink was strong and tangy with fresh lime. As good as the margaritas I mixed. Maybe that was just the heat talking. I examined the man across from me—the strong jaw, the muscles, the trim haircut with flecks of gray around the ears. What the fuck was I doing? I commanded myself to relax. I was just having dinner. What did I think I was doing? He had invited me. What was I supposed to do? Go to the next restaurant over and eat? Moon around and stay single until David Shapiro threw aside his demands and worshipped at my feet?

I was overreacting. At the moment, Mark did not even seem that interested in me. He observed the passersby.

"Are you looking for someone?" I asked.

"You might say that."

I was saying that. I was asking that. His answer annoyed me. I liked people to be more direct. Blunt even. Like my mom. I swallowed hard, took a big gulp of margarita, and choked.

Mark jumped up, patted me on the back, and handed me a glass of water. "Drink some of this."

Geez. He probably thought I was some pantywaist who couldn't handle a stiff drink. My skin began to prickle. Now that I had his full attention, I was about to commence perspiring like a basketball player. I held my margarita to my forehead.

When Mark was reseated, a little girl in a purple velvet dress and bare feet appeared at our table. She extended arms hung with necklaces of shells and silver and beads. In her hands she held tiny brightly painted porcelain animals.

Mark shook his head, but I smiled, happy for the distraction. Even in her heavy dress, the little girl appeared cool, two immaculate braids hanging down her back, not a trace of sweat on her smooth brown face. She placed a blue, yellow-spotted rhinoceros on our table and regarded us with dark, solemn eyes.

If we picked up the treasure, it was as good as sold.

Mark shook his head again and flicked his hand. The child reclaimed her rhino and left. The waiter arrived with my food and my hormones relaxed. The tortillas were hot and fresh, the snapper swimming in a spicy red sauce with vegetables.

Mark watched in morbid fascination as I wolfed my food. I forced myself to reduce the amount of fish on my fork, but it kept increasing.

He smirked.

"I'm starving," I protested.

"I can tell."

I blushed, and tried again to shovel daintily. I chewed thoroughly before asking, "So what are you doing in Zihuatanejo?"

"Vacationing."

"I don't believe you."

He shrugged. His eyes searched the promenade. "What kind of work do you do, Carol?"

My stomach was finally beginning to register fullness. "I'm a baker."

When David Shapiro laughed, he only made sarcastic little barks. Mark Escalante had a full-throated laugh. It would have sounded delightful, except he was laughing at me. I patted my mouth with my napkin.

"Nothing wrong with being a baker," he said, "I just wouldn't have guessed it in a million years."

I peered around for the waiter. Where was the check when you needed it? Instead of the waiter, I spotted the woman from the plane, the blonde who had chatted up Mark, dressed now in an elegant sleeveless eyelet blouse, a straw hat and tortoise-shell shades. Nothing could hide her petite perfection. She sat, sipping an iced tea, nonchalantly studying us, with a video camera parked on her table.

I didn't care. Fuck it. She could have Mark. I didn't want to discuss making croissants. Especially not with someone who laughed at the idea. I wanted my room, a shower, and time to reflect on my meeting with Geraldo Sabala.

Mark took another sip of his drink and regarded me. "Hey, your guy looked familiar." There was something too casual in the remark.

"Geraldo Sabala?"

"Yes, Geraldo Sabala." He licked his lips as though tasting the name.

I had the horrible feeling that I had walked into an ambush, that Mark Escalante had been waiting to rehear the name, that the whole invitation to join him had been to snare this prey. I studied his face, but it was as impassive as a brick wall. I felt an impulse to bolt.

"Want the check?" Mark asked. He held up his hand and gestured brusquely.

A waiter appeared immediately. Mark ordered coffee in his flawless Spanish.

"¿Uno?"

"Sí. Y la cuenta por la señora."

Now I felt angry that he hadn't asked me if I wanted coffee, that he hadn't given me the opportunity to decline or to reject him. Even though I'd given every indication I wanted to go, it felt humiliating to be dismissed. I drained my drink and crunched an ice cube.

"I'm going to hang out," he said. "Enjoy the evening breeze. If you're in a hurry, you can leave the money. Ten bucks would be fine."

CHAPTER 11

In the cab ride to Villas Rosa, I vacillated between infuriation at Mark Escalante's dismissal and excitement about my intention to visit Geraldo Sabala the next day.

I should have told Mark that I was a P.I., not a baker. On the other hand, I was glad that I had withheld information. The guy had gone all day without revealing a thing about himself. Why had he wanted to know Geraldo's name?

My heart bubbled at the thought of my newfound brother, but I pushed the feeling aside for a full-scale pout in the back seat of the taxi. During my short walk to catch a cab, I had spotted three different people from the plane. Zihuatanejo was a good-sized town of about 60,000, but the tourist crowd milled within limited confines. Just from my initial stroll, the demarcation seemed as clear as a fence. The tourist area ran about seven blocks long and three blocks deep. I had been deluding myself to think Mark Escalante was following me. Folks from my flight had probably been streaming down Paseo del Pescador; I just didn't recognize all of them.

The taxi driver and I rode with the windows open, up over a grand hill to the area called La Ropa Beach, so named for a Chinese shipwreck that had sent clothes washing up on shore.

At a fountain of four dolphins, we turned toward a sunset that washed Mark and Geraldo away into a watercolor of peach and pink.

Villas Rosa perched on a hill, a street back from the beach, a family-run hotel with only a few units enclosed in a lovely garden of palms, hibiscus, and bougainvillea. The flora was young and newly planted, but promised to mature into a magnificent paradise.

A short, gray-haired lady with a dimpled smile rose from a hammock. She turned out to be Rosa herself. At an open-air office, I registered and paid for my first night. Rosa was joined by her equally short husband, a trim man in tan slacks, white *guayabera*, and sandals, who offered to carry my bag. I declined, but introduced myself, and in a short conversation, learned that he was a retired professor.

I struggled to open the heavy wooden door into my room, but once inside, I felt immediate relief. The room was tiled, clean, and Spartan with colorful floral curtains and bedspread. I stripped my clothes and took a long, weak, tepid shower. For a couple of minutes I admired my view out over the bay to the dark blue and tangerine remnants of the sunset.

Then I turned on the ceiling fan and climbed, naked, into the fresh sheets. A gecko zipped across the stucco wall and disappeared through the crack over the heavy door. I picked up the pink envelope my mother had left me. Pink. Feminine and romantic. It was so unlike my mother, at least the woman I had known. And the name of my father wasn't in her printing. The characters looked childish. I pressed along both sides with my fingers. I'd already rumpled the envelope with my curiosity. My fingers once again encountered only the sponginess of paper. The smallness of the envelope and the thickness of the contents suggested a creation that had grown out of control, like a jasmine vine or a cancer.

I flipped it over. The back had been practically and unceremoniously sealed with duct tape. Now, that was my mom.

This is for him.

The words didn't motivate the trip. She had written them already knowing I would go on this pursuit. My mom had known me better than anyone on earth.

But what would I do with the package if my dad was dead? It didn't seem likely that he would be dead of natural causes. Mom had died young and he was three years younger.

I picked up the photograph. The ceiling fan cranked lazily above me, like time itself, turning, turning. I fell asleep with the lights on, holding on to my dad.

CHAPTER 12

It did not matter that he had a minivan with stolen Arizona plates. Any car would look suspicious passing through the barbed-wire border fence. Any car would look suspicious driving across the open desert. Any car would look suspicious traveling at night along the dirt road of a cattle ranch.

Still Coyote Gee drove slowly. This work would be all for nothing if they died in a stupid accident.

After they had peeled back the barbed wire, they had rearranged themselves, with Ricardo and the curly-headed young man in the front with him, so he had six eyes to scan the dark desert. When the road veered away to the west, Coyote Gee continued across pasture land. Follow the Big Dipper constellation, he told himself, the drinking gourd, just as slaves had once followed it north.

Tension smoldered in the vehicle, as though the air itself were becoming thick and impenetrable. They all were probably thinking about the robber crammed in the corner. Coyote Gee clenched his jaw until his bad molar ached. He could forgive himself for the knife snuck on by the father of the family. Knives were thin and easy to conceal. The man may have had it tucked in his wife's underwear, and there were some places Coyote Gee would not pat. But he had missed the gun. . . . Even though it was a slim Firestar with a single-stacked magazine, it bothered him. Where had the robber stashed it? Maybe he was getting too old for this work.

But Coyote Gee smiled slightly at the image of the man bound with duct tape. Every man, he thought, had a magic tool. For some men it was a hammer. They could knock out dents, rip out walls and defend themselves as long as they had a hammer. Others might go for a length of rope. They could plumb a line, pull a heifer, or hang someone with a rope. For Coyote Gee, the talisman was duct tape. With duct tape a man could cinch up a dragging muffler, insulate a bare wire, or gag and bind a no-good son-of-a-bitch.

They could hardly have left him for the *Federales* to find, and if they dumped him on this side, he might choose to cooperate with U.S. Immigration if there was no gain otherwise. So for now he was bound in the back of the van.

No one spoke, so when Lupita said, "*¿Papi?*" Coyote Gee startled.

"Shhhhhhh," her papa said.

The inquisitive, half-frightened voice in the dark stirred a memory in Coyote Gee. He pictured his little boy on the table clutching his father's abandoned cup of *rompope*. Little Donald had spilled half of it down his pajamas, but had drunk most of it. It had been mixed stout, the way he liked all his drinks back then, but was still sweet enough to appeal to a child. Coyote Gee had woken from one of his stupors to find Donald there, and the little boy had looked up to him in a daze and said, "*¿Papi?*"

His heart clenched at the thought of his first son. He would be a grown man now, but as American as his name. He would no longer recognize his *Papi*.

Coyote Gee took a package of gum from his chest pocket and extended his arm to the back. "*¿Chicle?*"

Without a sound, the girl extracted a piece, careful not to touch him. He placed the package in the cup holder. He heard the rustle of the paper and the smacking of the first resistant, sugary chews. He smelled the mint and smiled to himself, vicariously lost for a moment in the child's simple pleasure.

Coyote Gee snapped back to focus on the desert. He had talked to his clients about the dangers of the desert and of *La Migra*, and they had experienced first hand the real scum—the *banditos* who roved the border to rob, and in other instances, to rape.

But Coyote Gee had not mentioned the rancher, a crusty old devil who was sick to death of immigrants, of the water bottles and abandoned bicycles and feces littering his sagebrush. Coyote Gee thought of the rancher as Mike, a name like a fist, a forceful, American name, so unlike Mexican names that took three syllables and sounded girly, names like Vicente, Concepción, and Geraldo. Mike, the rancher, was smart, but anger interfered with his thinking. Hunting for illegals, he took his rifle and drove his pickup down to the border on a regular basis. He never seemed to consider that he was being watched, and that in his hunt, he revealed the best path across his ranch.

In spite of his blind spots, Rancher Mike was to be taken seriously. He would use the rifle. Coyote Gee knew this first hand. He imagined the rancher could hit whatever he aimed at—he'd once blown out Coyote Gee's tire—but he'd sent the other bullets whizzing over their heads. That little adventure had convinced him to trade in his noisy truck for a minivan. He even took the precaution of putting an AVIS frame around the plates. This was a sparsely populated area and Rancher Mike and *La Migra* knew the locals' vehicles. But they also put up with the occasional crazy tourist, the obsessed bird watcher trying to spot a rare owl. If the rancher or *La Migra* got close enough to see the frame, they would probably already be in trouble, but you never knew. You never knew what small detail might save your ass.

Peering into the dark, Coyote Gee made out the darker dark of the jagged mountains.

This route, north from Sasabe, zigzagging a path near 286 until he found his entrance point to the highway, was known as Cocaine Alley. Mike, the tough stringy rancher, was angry and disgusted enough to shoot at Coyote Gee's cargo, but Mike would look like a *mariposa* compared to the drug runners. Drug runners would just shoot them.

CHAPTER 13

Climbing the stone steps at the end of La Ropa Beach, I conceded that I'd made a horrible mistake by walking to town. I had decided to explore my surroundings en route to see Geraldo Sabala. As sweat poured down my forehead, I fully appreciated why people took siestas, why Geraldo Sabala had not been busy the previous afternoon, and why tourists crowded the taxi station down the street from Villas Rosa. It was only ten in the morning and the temperature felt like it had already hit ninety degrees.

My braided ponytail switched and slapped like a cow's tail as I labored up eighty-four stone steps. The steps didn't end the climb, but rather stopped at a steep service road up to the highway.

At the top I mopped my brow with Mark Escalante's sock. I had borrowed scissors from Rosa and taken great pleasure in cutting it open. I tucked the improvised hanky back into the waistband of my shorts.

At least the climb had been in shade. On the highway to town, the sun blazed in full glory. Smoke from burning garbage or a field being cleared rose from a distant hill. It curled like an incantation: welcome to the tropics.

The narrow sidewalk was on the wrong side of the road for signaling a cab and the other side had no shoulder to speak of. I trudged over the crest of the hill, watching my feet as much as the vistas, since the sidewalk had a way of dropping suddenly or disintegrating into crumbles of concrete.

It was just as well. I couldn't have concentrated on the

views, anyway. My mind was full of what I would say to Geraldo Sabala. I had so many questions, I was afraid of over-whelming him. And I had to steel myself for the answers, answers I already suspected: No, he never mentioned you. Or your brother. Or his other wife. My heart hammered in my head. Of course, all this depended on if Geraldo Sabala would even talk to me.

Worse yet, the whole thing could be a coincidence. But what were the chances? Here was a guy with my father's name, in my father's hometown, who looked a lot like my brother Donald. Private investigators only believed in coincidence as a last resort. "When you have eliminated the impossible," Sherlock Holmes said, "whatever remains, however improbable, must be the truth."

On the other side of the hill, I cut through a hotel to find steps down to La Madera Beach, which meant The Wood Beach. My tourist literature explained that wood had once been loaded on ships here. This beach was shorter than La Ropa, with hard-packed dark sand. I followed a wooden walkway into Zihuatanejo. I crossed the Canal Agua de Correa, an ironic name since the canal did not contain a drop of running water. The bridge was painted the same ochre with terra cotta trim as the seawall and tiers at the plaza.

In relief, I found myself strolling along the shaded espla-nade of Paseo del Pescador.

"Hey, Carol."

Mark Escalante sat at the exact table where I'd left him. I might have thought he'd never moved except his luggage was gone and he was wearing shorts, Hawaiian shirt and tan base-ball cap. The whole tourist garb, including a black fanny pack that he had laid on the table.

"*Hola*," I greeted him.

He motioned me over. He glowered at my waist.

I glanced down.

"Isn't that my sock?"

"Didn't you give it to me?"

"Didn't you say there was nothing sadder than a single sock?"

"They're divorced now."

"So it committed *hara kiri*?"

I smiled. Black humor was my type. I told myself that my previous hurt feelings had more to do with my ego than anything Mark had done. At the moment, with hula girls adorning his chest, he seemed relaxed and approachable.

"Like to sit?" Using a leg, he pushed out a chair. *Semper Fi* tattooed his calf.

Behind the dark Bucci's, I sensed boredom and suddenly it all made sense—the goofy clothes, the set location, the watching, the lingering over coffee. I felt a surge of sympathy. Mark Escalante was on a stakeout.

I perched on the edge of a chair. "Are you a private investigator?"

He looked at me quizzically. "There's nothing worse than a private dick."

"Oh." That stung worse than his response to my job as a baker. I wasn't going to wait around to be laughed at and dismissed again. I had better things to do. "I gotta go."

We needed to continue this little conversation. But later would be fine. I knew where to find him.

Geraldo Sabala came eagerly from the kitchen when I arrived. "*La Loca*," he greeted me with a smile.

This portended well. Something had shifted.

Only one customer graced the joint, the same young shirtless guy who had been there the day before. He sat at the same outside table, drinking another Corona. A regular. Even Archibald's, the fancy restaurant where I baked, had regulars, couples who pilgrimaged there every Sunday and worshipped at the same window seat.

"Could we talk?" I asked.

Geraldo indicated one of the two inside tables, in the

corner near the window, an instinctive or practiced choice where he could view the outside, the door, and the kitchen all at once.

"Would you like something to drink?"

That sounded heavenly.

"¡M'ija!"

The daughter trotted out from a hidden part of the kitchen and over to our table. I ordered lemonade and he told her to bring him a Coke.

"There are many reasons I wish not to discuss my father," he began.

"Didn't you like him?"

Geraldo drew back. "He was a great man."

The past tense again. As much as I did not want to accept this outcome, I had known from the outset that my father could be dead. I focused now on the man across the table, fiddling with his mustache. Call me Dr. Phil, but when people did not respond directly, I sensed conflict, but I let his response sit for a moment. "I'm sure he was. What did he do?"

Geraldo tapped the table. The daughter brought our drinks, carried aloft on a tray. After she set them on the table, her father shooed her away like a fly. This man may have looked like Donald, but he certainly did not act like him, but then Donald was gay, and this man was a macho Mexican. He had darker, harder eyes.

"That is something I wish not to discuss."

I wondered what the guy was willing to discuss and why, if his father was such a touchy subject, he had decided to be friendly to me. I removed my small, shoulder strap money pouch and took out the photo. I slapped it on the table like an ace of spades. "This was my father."

He sucked some Coke before leaning over to scrutinize the photo. He picked it up and held it close to his eyes as though he were near-sighted.

"Who is the woman?"

"My mother. His wife."

Geraldo Sabala laughed. "This is not my father."

CHAPTER 14

I sat paralyzed for a moment, feeling hope drain out of me. I sipped my lemonade, which in Mexico meant limeade, the taste bright and sharp. My fingers quivered against the glass. "Why do you say that?" I imagined that Geraldo Sabala's father had been a foot taller, somehow distinctly not the man in the photo.

"My father never had another wife," he declared indignantly.

"That he told you about," I retorted.

Geraldo looked confused. I repeated myself in Spanish, a little more politely.

"My father loved my mother," Geraldo insisted. He squinted at the photo. "My father had a scar on the side of his face."

"People can get scars any time in their lives."

Geraldo laid the photo on the table and tapped it. "And this baby. That's you?"

I nodded. "And the little boy is my brother Donald."

He leaned over and studied Donald, frowned, and rubbed his fingers over his lips. He picked up the photo again and sipped his cola. "Donald?" he repeated. He squinted at the photo, turned it for better light.

After a couple of minutes, he slid back the photo. He set down his drink and scratched his hair. "You tell me about this man. Your father. Maybe he was a cousin to my dad." He shrugged. "Cousins sometimes have the same name."

I had to admit this possibility. Even though the man sitting across from me shared my brother's thick eyebrows, strong nose, and square jaw, second cousins could look surprisingly alike, although Donald would not have been caught dead in brown polyester slacks. Genes mixed and matched in mysterious ways. Or didn't swap around much at all. I had inherited my mother's looks intact while my brother had inherited our dad's.

It didn't take me long to tell Geraldo everything I knew about my father, how he worked as an illegal immigrant in the Ferndale area, married my mother, bore two children, fled the United States during the time of Operation Wetback, and disappeared from our lives.

"Why did he leave?" Geraldo asked. "If he marries an American, then he probably has a green card."

My arm froze mid-lift. Yes, wasn't that true? Didn't some people get married just to obtain green cards? Maybe my father had never returned because that was the only reason he married in the first place. After all, how common was a mixed marriage back then?

But I answered, "I don't know if they had green cards during the fifties, and even if a person had one, I'm not sure Operation Wetback cared."

A group of three young white males plopped down at an outside table. They had their shirts open and their baseball caps on backwards so as to be sure not to get skin cancer on the napes of their necks. Geraldo's daughter was already hurrying toward them.

Geraldo stood, taking his Coke with him. "They will want pizza. Pepperoni, I bet." He smiled and my brother Donald leapt out of his skin like a stripper from a bachelor party cake. "Lots of beer," he added happily.

I followed him across the small room. "I'd like to talk to you some more."

"Of course," he said. "You could be *mi prima*."

His cousin. He had completely distanced himself from the idea we might share a father, that I might be his half-sister. Yet, something had changed; perhaps he had seen himself in little

Donald's face. "This is a good time of day," he said. "*Mañana.*" He passed through the counter door and strapped on his apron. "Or any day." He reached into a cup on the counter and handed me a business card. "This man you want, though, is not my father."

"How can you be so sure?"

"My father would never leave his family."

CHAPTER 15

As much as I harangued about the corporate invasion of quaint places, I found myself wishing for an Internet Café. The closest thing Geraldo could offer was ZihuaRob, an American English-as-a-Second-Language teacher who was attempting to usher Zihuatanejo into the looming twenty-first century.

ZihuaRob lived one street back from the beach in his wife's family home, a yellow building with maroon awnings, at the corner of Juan N. Alvarez and Vincente Guerrero. His wife's clothing shop and ZihuaRob's office occupied the bottom, Geraldo had explained.

"If the office door is locked, knock hard. He's probably in the back giving an ESL lesson."

Following directions, I pounded on the door. A tanned guy in sandals, shorts and light blue *guayabera* answered the door. He had brushed-back brown hair and the white straight-toothed smile for which Americans are famous the world over. He greeted me with a Southern accent and the smell of patchouli oil.

He knew immediately what I wanted, quickly set me up at one of his computers, told me what he charged, and then ducked through a Hobbit-sized door in the back of his office and disappeared.

I stared at the small door. That and the quickness of the exchange left me with a sense of unreality.

Seated awkwardly at the computer, I stared at the screen, even though I was paying by the minute. I had never wanted to, and therefore never did, fully believe our father had simply deserted us. Slowly, I typed a search for Operation Wetback. Or more accurately, why my father might have fled even though he was the spouse of an American and could have applied for a green card, a permanent visa. Possibly he hadn't applied, but as a citizen's husband, it seemed like he would occupy a more elevated status than illegal immigrant, that a crackdown would have spared him.

As I clicked on the most promising link and read the information, relief washed over me. It didn't take long to get a sense of the threat my father might have felt. Between 1949 and 1953, the number of illegal immigrants captured at the border had more than tripled from 280,000 to 865,000. This resulted in Operation Wetback, which cast a wide net and included local police, to capture "illegal aliens." The program tended to target all Mexicans. The police invaded barrios and in some cases, American-born children were deported along with illegal immigrants.

I seized the idea. My father had left to protect us.

I stood from the desk and stretched. ZihuaRob had not returned. The rabbit-hutch door suggested mysterious, forbidden realms, so I left my money by the computer and saw myself out.

My head spinning, I walked away from the beach and crossed Benito Juarez, a main thoroughfare, and a clear boundary between tourist territory and the "real" town. Here a man sold bags of limes from the back of his battered truck and a girl ladled *horchata* and orange juice from large jars in her bicycle cart. A narrow, dark store cranked out tortillas and a counter displayed chopped chicken with another young girl indolently fanning away the flies. Vegetable stands pulled the eye to heaps of peppers, tomatillos, avocados and Roma tomatoes. After batting away clothing strung low over the sidewalk, not marketed to tall Americans like me, I decided to walk in the street. Then, a little worried I might get lost on these byways named after coconuts, mangos and oranges, I doubled back to

Benito Juarez. In the mess of traffic, a truck, so old its original color was lost, towed a flatbed bearing a corralled camel. A speaker mounted on the cab of the truck blared indecipherable Spanish, as a little boy ran behind the flatbed and darted onto the sidewalk to sell tickets. The seated camel absorbed the commotion with unmitigated lethargy. I hailed a cab.

Back at La Ropa, I walked the beach, carrying my sandals and a lighter heart.

My father had wanted to keep us safe. Given the times, maybe the government would have deported his wife and children along with him. They would have taken one look at my brother Donald and seen him as a brown-faced threat to the future economic prosperity of America.

The warm lapping water at my feet offset the blazing sun and was perfect for ruminating. Why hadn't my father taken us with him? I smiled at the thought of growing up here, speaking Spanish, lounging lazily at the Town Square, sucking at a straw stuck into a *coco frio*, watching handsome young men play basketball at a netless rim.

Cutting through the hotel Villa Mexicana, I used their footbaths to clean the sand from my feet and spotted yet another couple from the plane, reading paperbacks under the hotel's *palapas*. On the street behind the hotel, a mangy dog with pink eyes and protruding ribs ripped at a plastic garbage bag spilling fish heads and disposable diapers on to the cobblestones. The fetid, rotten, rich stench hung in the air.

When I was safely ensconced in my room, I collapsed on the bright floral bedspread. The ceiling fan stirred the air.

My mom, I was certain, would not have wanted to go to Mexico. She was descended from Protestant, mid-America stock. She did not speak Spanish and had never visited Mexico. It probably had been shocking enough that she married a Mexican. She had portrayed us as deserted, but maybe she had, as she would say, "put her foot down." With her white skin, my mother had no reason not to believe in American justice.

CHAPTER 16

Coyote Gee had driven for a half hour. The stars dazzled the dark sky like glitter on black paper. He had turned off the air-conditioner and the air through the window smelled sweet and pure. The *norteamericanos* even called the nearby area Buenos Aires National Wildlife Refuge. Good air. He sucked in deeply, trying to inhale the peace, the refuge.

But his insides roiled. No matter how many times he smuggled people, he thought of nothing else for days before the trip. Now, his heart raced at every rough bump. He had seen a pick-up abandoned out here with a broken axle. He had seen a bicycle with a bent tire left in the middle of nowhere. If anything happened to the vehicle, they were screwed.

Coyote Gee charged one thousand dollars a head, five hundred up front and five hundred when they reached their destination. He was cheap compared to the going rate, but then some of the coyotes were full-service, supplying the phony ID's and even jobs on the other side. He merely transported his clients to a safe house near Three Points where they could consider their options.

The safe house had belonged to an anti-immigrant Republican rancher, so even though he had died and left the place to his no-good son, as long as the son maintained the rifles in the back of his truck and cursed the filthy beaners, the house fell outside the INS radar.

From the house, his clients were on their own to move east to Tucson or west to California or maybe north to the packing plants of Kansas. To run blowers, pick strawberries, or hack up cattle in one hundred degree heat was the end game. Coyote Gee would stake all the money of this run that none of the people in his van believed the United States was the land of milk and honey. Most of them had left their wives and children at home with a few pigs, a cow or two, and maybe some chickens, left them in a shack, so they could go north to make money, because NAFTA had dried up farm subsidies.

The men had no choice but to go north. What good man would not do something illegal to feed his family? Yet, Coyote Gee thought bitterly, the people who hired them and exploited them would be the first to blame them for everything wrong with America. If the Americans really did not want these men, they did not need more INS or better fences; all they had to do was stop offering work. It was that simple.

CHAPTER 17

I woke from an involuntary siesta feeling ravenous, and vengeful toward the cocky, superior Mark Escalante. I was proud to be a private investigator, and I could be pretty damn alluring when I put my mind to it.

After a shower, I wrapped in a towel and unpacked my suitcase, looking for something that might qualify as elegant, or at minimum, cute, even though I knew the depressing contents of my pack—the Levi's from the plane, two pairs of cotton shorts, and various tee-shirts. A longing for David rushed through me. He thought I was hot even in bubble-butt bicycle shorts.

I slipped on my black cotton shorts, black sleeveless cotton shirt and Teva sandals. Dabbing on a bit of make-up, I left my hair wild and loose and headed for the beach. Behind the restaurants and hotels were little shops. I found a clothing store with a display of batik wraps—*pareos*. Picking one of brilliant blues, I looked into a mirror, and held the fabric to my face.

"It accents your eyes," the young sales clerk told me. She spoke good English. "It's a pretty color with the red in your hair."

"I've seen people wear these, but I don't know how to do it," I confessed.

"Do you want a dress or a skirt?"

"Dress?"

The girl shook out the cloth, folded down a small section, coiled the ends, wrapped it around me, asked me to lift my hair, and expertly tied it around my neck. "Nice, huh?"

"Can you make it shorter?"

She smiled knowingly and repeated the process as I watched

intently. It reminded me of coiling dough for Danishes.

I studied myself in the mirror. "Let me try it without my other clothes on."

"Certainly."

In the dressing room I awkwardly repeated the girl's movements.

"Are you doing okay?" she asked.

"Just a minute." I had the coiled ends in each hand and hadn't thought about my hair. I whipped and tipped my head, but my heavy hair hung like a wet towel. My skin prickled with frustration and embarrassment. I yanked the fabric to tie it and pulled hair along with it.

"Do you need some help?"

"Let me try again."

I put the *pareo* aside, plucked strands of my hair from the fabric, and dried my face with my shorts. I twisted my hair into a loose braid and draped it over a shoulder. The second try went better. I stepped out of the dressing room and inspected myself in the mirror.

"That looks great," the clerk said. She sounded very sincere.

I smiled at her salesmanship, but the effect was good—casual but sexy, the flap like a slit in a dress, promising to reveal flashes of flesh as I moved. The color did set off my eyes.

"I'll wear it home."

Even I knew the Teva sandals didn't work with the outfit, so I walked out to the beach in my bare feet, carrying a plastic bag full of my clothing and a sheet of directions, showing about twenty different ways to wear a *pareo*. The warm, calm water lapped at my toes, and desire tugged at me to float on the peaceful surface, to look up at the sun and forget about everything. By the time I had finished walking, the sun was starting its descent and the white Christmas lights twisted up the trunks of the palms blinked on.

I made a pit stop at the hotel to drop off the bag, touch up my makeup, and scrub my dirty feet. What I needed were some stiletto come-fuck-me sandals. What I settled for were clean feet and a pair of flip-flops. I laboriously brushed out my hair and went to catch a cab.

Mark Escalante, here I come.

I knew where to find him. He was still at the same table. I felt a surge of sympathy. Stakeouts were the worst. My first job had been to spy on a guy's neighbor. Our client had hired my boss J.J. Sloan to watch his neighbor's construction project daily from eight to four to make sure the neighbor, who was supposedly building a non-habitable work space, didn't convert it into an illegal habitable building. J.J. hated this type of work, and had blessed me with all the hours of it I could manage. It was butt-numbingly dull.

But Mark had said there was nothing worse than a private dick. My sympathy evaporated. I had a score to settle.

Since he was scanning the strolling crowd, Mark quickly spotted me. As I approached his table, I savored the up and down flick of his eyes. I didn't wait for an invitation to sit.

I gestured with my head toward the blonde woman. "Has she been here all day, too?"

Mark shrugged.

"Oh, come on. An observant guy like you. What is she doing? Staking you out?"

"Have a seat, Carol," Mark said sarcastically. "Make yourself at home." The hula girls on his blue rayon shirt had wrinkled and sagged.

"I'm hungry, and I have a bone to pick with you." I heard my voice using one of my mother's clichés. Sadness coursed through my body as though in my blood, pumped out by a wounded heart. I regretted every time I had made fun of her clichés, every time I had been less than a perfect daughter. My whole life, essentially.

Since only a few tables were full, a young, thin man with a sliver of mustache, cruised right over. I ordered a beer and the same meal I had eaten the night before. Why fool with success? He smiled and looked hopefully at Mark, but he shook his head.

I silently watched the sunset for what seemed like a half hour, but was probably five minutes. Let Mark wait and wonder. I loved the extra hour of daylight and the extended twilight offered by being this far south.

Mark glanced at the petite blonde woman who in turn shot flamethrowers at me.

"Do you know her?" I asked.

"She was on the plane with us."

"I know that. You haven't answered the question."

"She's a videographer."

"You still haven't answered the question."

"Didn't you say you were a baker?"

"You still haven't answered the question."

"Stop the broken record, Carol. It's not going to work."

"So you do know her. From before you met her on the plane."

He kept his face non-committal, his steely eyes on the passersby. "You ask a lot of questions for a baker."

"And no one spends a vacation at the same table in the same restaurant twenty-four, seven."

"You do exaggerate. Two days." He held up two fingers in case I was deaf or slow. "It's a pleasant spot to hang out. See that guy?" He nodded toward a dark-skinned Neptune sitting in a rocking chair. "He runs snorkel trips in the morning and he's been right here, same time, same station, both afternoons, drinking beer and mescal."

"He's a local, not a tourist."

Our squabble was interrupted by the delivery of my meal, complete with a basket of warm tortillas, an icy glass, a cold beer and a plate of sliced limes. I crushed a lime on the top of the bottle and took a long swig. So much for my new ladylike appearance, but pouring beer into a glass ruined it.

"My new guess—BEA." Bail enforcement agent. I had only met one in my time with J.J. Sloan's Investigative Services, but I had the impression they were a button-down breed, people who acted within the strictly defined parameters of their profession, which did not include pursuing fugitives into Mexico.

"BEA?" he mocked. "For a baker, you sure have the cop lingo."

This would have come as a surprise to J.J. Sloan. Because I didn't use his terms like "perp" and "vic," he thought I talked like a "civilian." I wrapped a forkful of fish in a tortilla.

"I have another job," I confessed to Mark between mouthfuls. "I'm one of those despicable private investigators."

"Oh," he said. "So that's what ticked you off, my little comment about dicks being dicky?"

I nodded. "What don't you like about private investigators?"

"They're cocky assholes who get in the way."

"Of the bad guys." His words cut, but I had no time to lick my wounds. Mark's body tensed. His gaze pointed to a young man strolling toward the restaurant along the well-lighted esplanade. The man wore a wife-beater shirt, long shorts, and a backward baseball cap. Tattoos covered both of his buffed biceps. The man's head swiveled, like a flashlight picking a path. He turned his head to glance behind him.

Mark uncoiled from his seat. I'd seen his type of movement before in my cat Lola when she stalked a butterfly. Slowly, he unzipped his fanny pack and extracted a can of pepper spray and a pair of handcuffs. Wives, *esposas*, they called cuffs in Spanish.

The woman from the plane moved from her table out to the walkway. She stood there and fiddled with her camera. She aimed it toward the Pacific. Just a tourist, taking in the beauty of the sunset.

Mark's target greeted the tanned Neptune in his rocker and called out to our waiter. A regular on his turf, unsuspecting, but still wary, glancing back down the esplanade.

I put some money on the table and stood up.

Mark shot me a warning glance. Stay back.

His target threaded casually through the mostly empty tables.

In high school, I was the kind who ran toward frantic shouts of, "Fight! Fight!" I wasn't about to miss out on action.

When the young man reached a spot where he was by himself, Mark pounced, but his prey scrambled into the maze of tables, knocking over a caned chair.

Mark gave chase, stumbled on the chair and ricocheted into another table. Its leg collapsed. Plates and glasses shattered on the tiles. The surprised diners, a couple, jumped up, the woman swiping at her sundress, and the man shouting angrily, "Jesus Christ, buddy!" Someone or something must have crushed cilantro; its scent dominated that of spilled beer and fish. I circled the tables in the opposite direction to where a handful of patrons had collected.

The waiters stood back, but a corpulent man in slacks and dress shirt, shouted at Mark and his quarry, first in Spanish and then in English, "Stop, you! Stop, you!" The young man zigzagged through the tables, and Mark pursued, leaving a path of destruction. The young man leapt onto a chair and sprang off the other side, kicking the wooden legs back toward Mark's shins. Mark hopped aside. They both looked practiced at foot chases.

But neither had given a thought to me. I stepped out and cut off the young man's escape route. If he wanted to reach the sidewalk, he would have to go through me.

And that was exactly what he intended to do. He lowered his head and charged, slamming into my side, and yanking down my *pareo*.

My body spun as his Oakland A's baseball cap flew onto the sidewalk, but my roadblock allowed Mark to latch on to the young man's shirt. When he turned toward Mark, Mark sprayed him in the face. After a stunned second, the man threw his hands to his eyes, cursing in Spanish and English between coughs. Pepper spray was like needles to the eyeballs. Mark pushed him to his knees, twisted the arms behind him, and cuffed him. Snot flowed down the captive's face.

People were too absorbed in all this to notice my bare breast, or so I hoped, as I quickly retied my wrap. A crowd had gathered, the petite blonde right in front with me, filming everything.

Mark grabbed the guy's hair and hoisted him to his feet, mucus flying onto his undershirt. The captured man kicked at Mark. Mark raised the can and quelled his attitude with the threat of a little more spray. I clutched my throbbing side and hoped that this crazed maniac hadn't cracked my rib. My eyes stung and my throat burned from the fallout of the spray.

The old Neptune man laughed drunkenly from his perch as though he hadn't seen anything this funny since the last Cantinflas movie. Some of the captured man's friends were shouting to him, asking the man, who seemed to be named Lalo, what was going on. They hung back though, unsure of Mark's authority and not wanting a taste of pepper spray. Our waiter, who had greeted Lalo on his arrival, clenched his fist and stepped forward. He'd probably like to punch Mark just on the grounds he had occupied a table for two days without ordering much. The owner grabbed the waiter's white jacket and pulled him back.

In spite of the chaos and my aching side, I smiled. The owner was acting just like Eldon, my kitchen manager in the states. You didn't want a customer to get cold-cocked in your restaurant; it was bad for business.

Grasping a fistful of shirt and holding aloft the small canister of spray, Mark calmly told the crowd in Spanish, "This man is a criminal wanted in the United States for a double murder. He killed his wife."

Lalo started coughing again, but the crowd looked less than sympathetic. They stared at him appraisingly and suspiciously, and then back at Mark with similar expressions. Mark marched Lalo through the parting crowd, out toward Juan N. Alvarez Street, as the police arrived in little white Nissan pickup trucks. The blonde, who had been following and taping, suddenly turned and beat a hasty retreat. Mark tossed the pepper spray into a potted plant.

The trucks screeched to a halt and officers jumped out of the cabs, leaving their doors open. They pointed shotguns at Mark and Lalo. Mark threw his hands in the air. Lalo turned so they could see the handcuffs. Tears streamed down Lalo's face. He tried to speak, but hacked instead. One officer grabbed Mark and another pulled Lalo by the arm. They shoved each into an individual pickup truck and ordered them to lie face down.

"*Y su novia,*" the young waiter said, pointing at me. He bobbed up and down in his excitement like a little kid.

"*Sí,*" the fat owner type confirmed. "She was fighting, too."

"I'm not his girlfriend," I protested, but a policeman had already gripped my arm.

CHAPTER 18

"Jesus, Carol, what the fuck?" Mark sputtered.

My face jounced against the metal of the truck bed. Each bounce blasted pain through my ribs. The pepper spray residue tickled a cough, which I squelched by imagining a blown-apart rib. The police here didn't need handcuffs. A cop sat on the side of the truck with an antiquated shotgun pointed at our heads.

"Don't start ranting. It's a waste of time."

"Couldn't you have just stayed out of things?"

"The waiter thought I was with you." I tried to move my hand slowly and carefully toward my face to cushion my head from the hard bumps over cobblestone.

"¡*Pare*!" Stop!

I froze.

"They would have arrested me even if I had stayed at the table."

"I don't think so," Mark muttered. "But, hey, you had to live down to my opinion of dicks."

"You wouldn't have caught your guy if it weren't for this private investigator."

"Like hell." Maybe part of him did appreciate me because he was silent for a moment, before he spoke again. "Mexican jail is no fun; you can't just post bail and leave."

"Why don't you tell me what's going on?"

"That Lalo punk shot and killed his wife and her lover and then fled to Mexico. The police haven't had any luck with extradition. Down here the attitude seems to be the wife had it coming."

The police officer shot us a dirty look. Wiggled his shotgun a little, but didn't tell us to shut up. He looked all of eighteen tucked into the officialdom of a blue shirt and dark fatigues. His combat boots planted in front of my face were as thin as the shoebox they came in. The hair trapped under my body yanked my scalp with every bump, so I rocked a little to loosen it.

"*¡Pare!*" The kid poked me with the gun.

I lay still. "My hair," I explained, rolling my eyes up to him.

He did his best to assume an I-don't-give-a-shit expression and let his eyes rove down to my legs.

"So where do you come in?" I hissed at Mark.

"The lover didn't have any money to speak of, but his family does. They're offering $100,000 for that piece of shit."

"You're a bounty hunter?"

After traveling for ten minutes, the truck had stopped.

"This may not be pure hell," Mark said dryly.

I didn't share his optimism.

With a wave of his shotgun, the lad of an officer indicated we should get out of the truck. Twilight was turning to dusk. We were parked in a big lot in front of a low, dirty stucco building. A faded sign indicated the facility was El Centro de Readaptacion Social, The Center for Social Readaption, one of those euphemisms like the Adjustment Center at San Quentin.

A stout female police officer emerged from the building as our officers unloaded us, jabbing Mark in the back with the shotgun. She wore the same uniform as her male counterparts, including the blue baseball cap that said: *Policia*, missing its accent mark. However, she had been endowed with a submachine gun.

"*¿Borrachos?*" the female officer asked. Drunks?

The older police officer who had been driving spoke in animated, rapid fire Spanish that was hard for me to follow except for the "*turistas locas.*" Crazy tourists.

The woman shook her head and considered both of us as though we had been very naughty children. There was no sign of the other truck containing Lalo.

Several gloomy little offices stood open to the parking lot. We marched into one. The walls and floors were concrete. There were two desks, one topped with an ancient manual typewriter and that was about all—no computers, no air-conditioning, not even a file cabinet for their paperwork. A male officer behind the desk asked us for our personal effects. I handed over my little money pouch, containing my passport, and the man noted my name, address, and birth date. He seemed beyond bored. He repeated the process for Mark, who carried his money and passport in the pocket of his tourist shorts.

So much for the special padded intake cell one might find in an American jail. The man didn't ask for our belts or shoes, but maybe he had noted neither of us wore belts or had shoes with laces. Or maybe Mexican jails didn't concern themselves with hangings.

"There's one hundred dollars in my wallet," Mark announced.

The four officers exchanged glances. The man behind the desk pursed his thick lips and eyed the wallet, but the woman shook her head vigorously enough to swing a ponytail of lush hair.

"Do you have any money?" Mark asked me.

"Only about twenty dollars."

"Not all Mexicans are for sale," the woman snapped. She had understood our English just fine. Her grip on the machine gun tightened, flexing her arm muscles.

"What happened to the other man you arrested?" Mark inquired as the young male officer patted him down.

They both widened their eyes at his Spanish. The boy shrugged.

"That man is a murderer wanted in the United States for a double homicide," Mark said. "There's an article about the murder and a copy of the arrest warrant in my wallet."

The older male officer simply smiled as though he enjoyed

watching his sturdy female counterpart pat me down.

"The hundred dollars," Mark mentioned again, "don't take it as *una mordida*. Take it as a gratuity to deliver this message to your superiors. The man I captured, Lalo de la Cruz, is wanted in the United States for a double murder."

This time the older man nodded solemnly instead of grinning.

"My capture has been caught on tape, and my partner is headed back to the United States, right now, with the evidence. Do not release him like he's just some drunk and disorderly."

The female officer joined our original two, and the three of them marched us back to the cells where we stared at the small dark interiors. These were not like the holding rooms in a modern jail with a strong door and a window of reinforced glass. These were old-fashioned barred cages. The older officer pushed Mark toward a dark pit. "*Y mi mujer*," Mark demanded. My woman. I guess he meant me.

"Is she your wife?" the older officer asked.

"*Si.*" Mark lied fluently.

"She has a different name."

"That's common in the United States."

The three had an elaborate powwow, with many references to *Americanos*, but finally pushed me into a dank hole across from Mark. It smelled like mold, like a place the sun never shone. I wondered if usually they had different cellblocks for men and women, but there was probably nothing usual about this arrest.

They left hesitantly, as though we had provided the best entertainment they could expect from the day.

As they walked away, we could hear the tone of argument, but not the words. "Good," Mark said. "Message delivered."

I clung to the bars, peering out, like some sad-sack cartoon of a prisoner. "What makes you think they won't just pocket the money?" My mouth was dry.

"Honor among thieves."

"Don't they allow us a phone call?"

Mark laughed. "Look at this joint. Did you even see a phone?"

"How do they communicate?"

"Didn't you see the radios on their belts?"

"They must have a phone."

"They probably do have one in some air-conditioned office for a muckety-muck wearing a suit."

I brushed off the grit from the truck and my torso screamed at me. I gingerly touched my rib. Could a person feel a fracture?

The woman stomped back between the cells and posted herself, as though she meant to guard us. She stood rigidly, fuming.

"You could ask her to use a phone," Mark said in pig Latin.

"I don't think now is a good time."

I looked around my room. There was nothing in it except me and benches along the walls. This room didn't even have a toilet. It was gloomy and dank, unventilated and warm at the same time. "Why did you say this might not be so bad?" I asked Mark.

"We're lucky. There are two systems of law in Mexico, one for Mexicans and one for tourists."

"So what happens to us?" I asked. "Do they keep us here until we're supposedly sober and then just let us go?"

"When they're ready. We'll probably have to go before the *Juzgado*, but with tourists, anything short of drug possession or murder is usually handled with a fine."

"Voice of experience?"

"Did you know the English word hoosegow is a corruption of *juzgado*?"

"Shut up!" the guard barked in English.

Yes, I thought. Shut up. I didn't know about hoosegows, and at the moment, I didn't care. I retreated to the back of the dark den because I needed to sit and collect myself. Here I was in a Mexican jail about to spend the night with a man I had set out to seduce. Yeah, I could tell myself I'd set out to give him a piece of my mind, but I hadn't dolled up for nothing.

I heard my mom's voice from the grave saying, "Be careful what you wish for." I argued with my dead mom, moving my lips like a mad woman, but no doubt desire could make a fool of us. Look where I was. Plus, any desire I had felt for Mark had vanished. My mouth was paste, my skin clammy, and my hair a tangled mass.

I glanced at our guard. If the woman allowed me a call, who would I turn to? Did I call David Shapiro or Geraldo Sabala?

David was a fighter, meticulous and thorough. When tracking down a new camera, he would research *Consumer Reports* and e-opinions. He would badger the owners of camera stores, and corner people taking snapshots. But his obsessive behavior applied only to his interests. When we were discussing baking, he couldn't be bothered to distinguish one nut from another. Everything was a peanut. "Give me the cookie with the chocolate chips and peanuts." It didn't matter if they were walnuts or almonds or filberts.

I wasn't sure right now whether David would spring into action for me as a meticulous strategist with a scorched earth policy or whether he regarded me as a peanut.

Geraldo Sabala, on the other hand, spoke Spanish and was here in Zihuatanejo.

A third option was to call my boss. Not Eldon, my kitchen manager boss, but J.J. Sloan, of Sloan's Investigative Services. He was, after all, a licensed private investigator, and an excellent one in his own mind. J.J. Sloan ranked as the vainest ugly person I'd ever met. His vanity was so strong it might surpass his alcoholism. The development of a paunch had caused him to take up running, which was seriously cutting into his drinking.

I walked to the front of the cage. Opposite me, Mark stood assessing his surroundings, a concrete hallway lined with jail cells. It lacked the fluorescent lights and over-waxed linoleum of an American prison. In the cell at a diagonal I glimpsed a small, silent indigenous man. Where did the row end and how many other cells contained eerily quiet inmates?

Pep-talking my courage, I decided I would talk to the angry woman with the submachine gun.

CHAPTER 19

Sound traveled in the crisp desert air. Coyote Gee instinctively glanced up, though he could not see anything.

But the whir was distinctive—a small plane.

His passengers stirred. Ricardo looked at him questioningly. *La Migra* did not use small planes. They used helicopters.

Ricardo started to ask a question.

"Shut up!" Coyote Gee snapped. The nervous sweat in his armpits bit like ants.

He didn't need the silence to hear. The plane was flying low and coming closer. Coyotes weren't the only ones to use these remote, flat, ranch roads.

As an old man, as a coyote, Coyote Gee had been praying to Juan Soldado, the folk saint. Juan Soldado was the name given to Juan Castillo Morales, falsely accused of the rape of an eight-year-old girl. He had been shot under *la ley fuga*, shot as a fleeing suspect, after being taken to a cemetery and given the chance to run to freedom. The blood of injustice seeped from his grave, and Juan Soldado had become the saint of border crossings. Coyote Gee had been extremely lucky praying to Juan Soldado. When he was younger, and prayed to the Virgin, he had been caught every time. He had never met anyone so unlucky.

As the drone of the plane increased, he mumbled a prayer, first to Juan Soldado, and then to the Virgin, for back-up. After all, long ago, if he had made it across, back to his first wife Bea, he never would have met the love of his life. Little Geraldo would not exist. Maybe in a twisted way he had been lucky.

Until now.

He thought of Bea and his babies. Bea's auburn hair and colored eyes. The Evening in Paris perfume that she would dab on her neck for him. So exotic. And then, almost guiltily, he pictured Maria, so young, her perfect, smooth brown skin and flashing teeth, her smell something entirely different, earthy as *maíz*, like being home. Was this what they meant about your life flashing before you?

The whir grew into a roar.

He slammed on the brakes. "Grenade!" he shouted.

He had taught them this word, hoping it would never escape his lips. The passengers grabbed their belongings and shoved and tumbled from the doors. They split and ran in different directions as the plane swooped low over the van.

Coyote Gee slipped his gun into his waistband and swung out the door. Then he heard the banging and remembered.

He stuck his head back into the vehicle. The robber was kicking his bound feet against the floor.

Pendejo. But young. Coyote Gee thought of his own son and how stupid he had been. *Los Estados Unidos* had been the Land of Opportunity, opportunity for trouble, but sometimes all you had to do was wait. Now his son was a married man with a child of his own.

The plane touched down, the wheels bouncing on the hard dirt.

Coyote Gee crawled back to the kid. He writhed and twisted against the duct tape, his eyes full of terror.

"Listen to me," Coyote Gee rasped. "If these guys catch us, the best thing to happen would be if they kill us. So don't even think about screaming when you lose your mustache, and when I run, you are going in the opposite direction. Understand?"

The man nodded and Coyote Gee ripped off the tape.

Boots clomped over dry clods of earth.

His hands shaking, Coyote Gee fumbled with the tape around the man's wrists. The duct tape was stuck to itself and twisted. He needed a knife. Something sharp.

Two voices traveled through the porous desert air. One was a gringo voice. The word *wetbacks*.

A cold chortle. "Grab the little ones."

CHAPTER 20

"She looks bored," I said to Mark.

Our guard had walked to the end of the hallway. "Probably tired," Mark whispered. "The cops here work twenty-four hour shifts."

I stared at the woman's uniform stretched tight across her broad back. She slipped into the evening air.

"Don't start feeling sorry for her," Mark continued in a low voice. "The Guerrero police are noted for their corruption." Our officer left. "I guess you've never heard of the *desaparecidos* from the *Guerra Sucia*, The Dirty War. There are still families in the state of Guerrero searching for missing relatives."

I'd heard of *desaparecidos*, the disappeareds, but had associated political kidnappings and killings with Central America, not this quaint tourist fishing village.

"People here regard cops as criminals with badges."

"Do you think Lalo is here? In one of these cells?" My attraction to Mark had disappeared into the musty air. He seemed like a cocky, muscular know-it-all with thinning hair.

"Sure. But he's not receiving the VIP treatment we are."

"Why's that?"

Mark snorted. "Look at us. White American tourists. Lalo has brown skin and looks like a punk. Prejudices about those things don't stop at the border. Besides, he's Mexican—Lalo de la Cruz."

Sucking on a *paleta*, our officer returned.

The Guerrero police might have a bad reputation, but how vicious could a woman sucking on a fruit pop be? She looked all of twenty-five.

"*Hola*," I said. "That looks delicious." Where had she gotten it? There did not seem to be any refrigeration in the building. The idea of a vendor with one of his little carts rolling by the big bad police station at dusk delighted me. "What flavor is it?" My mouth was too dry to salivate.

"*Fresa*." Strawberry.

She walked away where she could lick her fruit pop without the indignity of me watching her tongue.

"What do you think will happen?" I whispered to Mark.

"What I hope will happen is they'll deport that scumbag Lalo. Tomorrow they'll release us, and I'll be on the first plane back to the U.S. to collect my reward."

Our officer doubled back and threw her *paleta* stick on the concrete floor. I asked her name.

She hesitated, inspected my harmless *turista* garb and sweaty brow, and then offered, "Carmen."

"Do you know La Pizza?"

She scowled and tried to reclaim the distance between prisoner and officer, but her instinctive politeness would not let her ignore me. "Of course."

"Do you know Geraldo Sabala?"

The woman smiled, ever so faintly. "He's my . . . cousin."

"*¿De veras?*" Really? The officer had a smooth face and even though she didn't wear make-up, her eyebrows were plucked to a pencil line. She stood for a while in the heat and her boredom. She ran two fingers along the crease of her blue uniform shirt. Glanced at me, adjusted the strap of her machine gun, and finally offered, "My little sister and his daughter are good friends."

I "chatted her up" as David Shapiro would call it. And as a result, she didn't offer me a phone, but agreed to place a call to Geraldo.

I had no way to tell the time. I didn't wear a watch and if

I did, the police would have taken it. I perched on one of the benches and, across from me, Mark stretched out on the hard wood. The temperature settled into balmy warmth. My throat was parched. My rib throbbed. I gently probed with my fingers and found the contact point of Lalo's head. The beer I had drunk was now stretching my bladder to an ache. I contemplated the drain in the floor.

Mark Escalante had fallen asleep and was providing sound effects—little hog grunts with the intake and soft whistles with the out breath. It irritated me that he was able to sleep, yet the snoring was reassuring. I played a game where I matched my breath to his. In and out, life went on, even in a Mexican prison.

It felt like the dead of night when Geraldo Sabala showed up. He greeted Carmen with what seemed like an unending series of *saludos*: How was she? How was her husband? How was her baby? How was her mother? Her brothers and sisters? while I stared at the bottle of water in his hand.

Mark Escalante stirred at the commotion, sat up and stretched.

Carmen handed me the bottle of water as she and Geraldo continued to converse. In spite of my bladder, I chugged half of it before I even thought of Mark.

Geraldo jerked his thumb at Mark and asked Carmen, "Who's he?"

She spoke in animated Spanish that was too quick for me, but included the name Lalo several times, and a raised hand moving back and forth in front of Geraldo's face. I took this as a reenactment of Mark's pepper spraying. "But," she concluded, "I do not think they are husband and wife. I do not think they really know each other."

Mark smirked. He pointed at Geraldo. "I might know you, buddy."

Geraldo turned in his direction, but did not approach the bars. He frowned at Mark Escalante. "No, man, I don't think so."

"Can you get me out of here?" I asked Geraldo.

"Don't worry," he said to me. "No problem. You will be out in the morning."

He talked some more with Carmen, and left. I stared at the drain.

CHAPTER 21

Geraldo was true to his word. In the morning, the two officers from the previous evening returned. Sometime during the night, I had finally dozed, and I woke frowzy with sleep, my mouth pasty, my eyes gummy, my back and legs stiff, and my ribs shooting pain with every move. I chugged the remaining water in the plastic bottle.

The older officer motioned with his shotgun. "She can go."

Carmen opened the door of the cell. I slipped on my flip-flops and slapped my way to the desk to pick up my passport and my freedom. "What about him?" I asked Carmen.

"Your husband?" the older officer said with amusement. "To the *Juzgado*."

As I walked, disoriented, from the building into the bright sunshine, Mexican police milled about the large parking lot. There were way too many of them for the size of Zihuatanejo. They looked at me as if I were an escaped chimpanzee from a zoo.

I wanted nothing more than to take a taxi to Villas Rosa, have a long, hot shower, and drink a gallon of stout coffee, but I thought of the corrupt police and Mark Escalante and people who simply disappeared. Still, I lifted my arm for a taxi. Mark seemed confident he would be okay. Besides, I wasn't sure I even liked the guy.

Within a minute, one of the white taxis stopped and I asked for my hotel in La Ropa Beach. Because my nose wasn't pressed into the dirt of a pick-up bed, I was able to see where I had been. The backside of Zihua consisted of dirty stucco buildings offering car repair, and shacks with children peering from "windows" with no glass.

At Villas Rosa, I labored up the short hill and then up the stairs directly to my bathroom. Safe in my room, I took a shower and tried to nap, but I kept replaying my night in hell and juicing my body with shots of adrenaline. I resigned myself to being awake. I stared at the hypnotic ceiling fan. What would my mom think if she saw me squandering her money this way? She wouldn't be surprised, not even at my night in jail. After all, she had finagled her way into two of my investigations and had once bashed a killer over the head with a statue. To her, I would be "off on a lark."

The pain in my rib emanated from my heart as though the memories of my mother vibrated the bone. People offered all sorts of advice to help me "get through it," to overcome the sorrow: Work. Help others. Meditate. Drink herbal tea. Go off on a crazy quest to find my father. They seemed to think a person came out the other side of grief into a new day, the way immigrants crawled through tunnels and emerged into a circle of light. But I didn't believe a person ever emerged from grief. It settled into the heart and poked its confines with a red-hot pitchfork until the heart swelled, became roomier, and in contrast, the grief seemed smaller. That's the way it had been with my brother Donald.

I sighed and felt like crying. The sigh made my torso ache. This was my third day in Zihua and so far I had not had one lick of fun. This was supposed to be a vacation, too. I thought guiltily of Mark, but what could I do for him? He had talked like he would get out.

One person I did need to see was Geraldo Sabala--to thank him and to continue my quest. But it was too early.

Instead of more work, bobbing in salt water might be just the thing for my aching ribs. In Santa Cruz, the Pacific was cold with rolling waves, great for surfers in wet suits, but not for me. I wasn't a strong swimmer and I had almost drowned once in the Eel River. But the ocean here was glassy and warm.

I shimmied into my swimsuit, old shorts and Hawaiian shirt and tucked an estimated amount of American money into my pocket to pay for breakfast and snorkel gear. I walked down to the office to talk to Rosa's husband, the retired professor. He looked the part with his short gray hair and wire-rimmed glasses that slid down his nose as he read the newspaper.

The open-air office consisted of a desk under a thatched roof. "*Buenos dias*," I greeted the professor.

He and Rosa appeared so content in their paradise that I felt wistful. Would I ever find such peace with a partner?

Laying down his newspaper, he returned the greeting. I sat in one of the cushioned wicker chairs and asked in Spanish where one might snorkel.

The professor, with the kindness and patience of a teacher, explained in slow, clear Spanish how to find the path at the end of the beach that would lead me to Las Gatas, a lagoon created by a coral reef that stretched into the bay. A short, over-priced boat ride was a second option for getting there.

The earlier I went the smoother and clearer the water would be. But I needed sustenance first. I passed through the gate in Villas Rosa's wrought iron fence and followed the short bend in the road to Elvira's on the beach. I ordered coffee and granola, yogurt and fruit. Relaxing in the shade, I admired the calm surface of the water. My heart fluttered as I contemplated my snorkeling adventure.

The waiter brought me a mug of strong, fresh coffee and a huge plate of bananas, pineapple, papaya, and cucumber topped with a thin yogurt and dark granola. I ate in rapturous bliss. The burst of sweet, tangy pineapple. How different from my night in jail! The buttery texture of the papaya. How quickly life changed.

As I lifted a huge spoonful of granola, my body tightened, and the hairs on my neck rose. I marveled at the subliminal messages our bodies pick up, so we knew, for example, exactly when a person at a stoplight was inspecting us.

I lowered my spoon, rationed its load in half, and glanced around the restaurant. Two tables on the beach were occupied, one by a couple from the plane, but everybody seemed focused toward the water, not at the piggish eater back in the shaded part of the restaurant.

Taking a dainty bite of food, I scanned Patti's Cafe next door. I didn't see anyone I recognized. I didn't see anyone checking out my hot, single, forty-something self. There was no evidence of Mark Escalante.

I twisted around. A worker turned brusquely. He wasn't wearing the all white of the waiters, but he climbed the steps to the kitchen as though he belonged to the place.

I stabbed my last piece of pineapple. It was hard and bitter.

After paying for breakfast, I set off for my adventure, unable to shake the sense I was being watched.

The beach ended at a dirt road. After a hundred yards the road stopped at a path over boulders, slick and stained from washed-up boat oil. My left hand was encumbered with the snorkel gear I'd rented at the end of La Ropa Beach. Reaching down with my right, I cinched my Teva's tighter. A magazine advertisement for the sandals showed a guy running, leaping from rock to rock. I was about to put the claim to test.

The path forced me to choose between walking on wet rocks or clambering over boulders, no easy task while clutching mask and fins, but the choice was simple. Every year in Santa Cruz some clown thought the warning signs about slippery rocks didn't apply to him and was swept out to sea. There weren't any signs here, or any threatening waves, but I still climbed up and over the boulders. Brilliant yellow blossoms rained down on the dark rocks and garbage-strewn weeds. I peered up for the source, but couldn't see it. Below me, the water surged quietly. I rested for a moment, enjoying my solitude. Out over La Ropa Beach a boat was pulling a tourist up in a purple and yellow paraglider.

Granted I wouldn't be washed out to sea up here, but a fall could be equally perilous. I'd always thought the best way to kill a person would be with a swift push off a steep cliff. You just had to make sure the cliff was high enough and that the person didn't have a chance to grab hold of you, or anything else, for that matter.

Footsteps jarred me from my reverie. I whipped around. A boy of about twelve, wearing only red shorts, bounded over the rocks. Barefooted.

He passed me silently and swiftly. Until that moment, I had been very proud of my progress.

I labored onward for about ten minutes, emerged at a boat dock, and scampered down rocks to a small curved beach lined with ramshackle, open-air restaurants fronted with wooden and plastic lounge chairs. At this hour, the sand was raked clean and only a few families sat at the accommodations.

Books recommended that one not snorkel alone, so I was relieved to see a man and a woman floating near the reef. I slipped off the clothes covering my bathing suit and laid them on a rock. Wading into the warm water, I dipped my head, and pushed wet tendrils off my face. I spit on my goggles and rinsed them in the salt water. I put the mask over my head and adjusted the snorkel tube. One foot at a time, I tugged on the hard, cheap fins, and then set off.

No water leaked into the mask. Stroking with my arms reminded me that I had recently been butted in the ribs, but my legs were strong from biking. After a few kicks into the lagoon, I reached clear water and the secret world. Far below me, a trumpet fish floated by. Like staring into space, exploring the world underwater put life into perspective. I was such a small part of the universe.

I lifted my head out of the water to look for the other couple. They were heading through the surf at the end of the reef into the bay, a little too scary for me. I stuck my face back in the water and admired small darting iridescent blue fish, ugly puffers, and a school of what might have been snappers, flashing silver in the sunlight. On the white sand rested a mossy anchor, longer than most of the boats that entered this small harbor, washed here from a bygone era.

An eel popped his head from the coral and opened his jaws like a ferocious lion. He coiled among the rocks.

Close by, an engine of a small boat blapped. Near the reef, I was safe, but I raised my head anyway. The boat stopped between the shore and me. Its sole occupant wore a snorkel mask and black swim trunks. The young slim body dove into the water and swam toward me with sure strokes.

I removed my mouthpiece. "There's an eel over here!" I was glad to have another snorkeler in the water.

He propelled himself in my direction.

I didn't know the word for eel in Spanish. "*Una cosa intere-sante*," I tried.

He glided toward me like a torpedo. Clearly the only "interesting thing" to him was me.

My instinct was to try to stand up, even though standing on the coral would kill it. A sharp projection ripped my ankle and I looked down.

The man grabbed my head and pushed me under water. My snorkel submerged and I sucked in a mouthful of salty water. Flailing, I grabbed at his body. Air. I needed air.

I latched on to his wrist. He put his feet on my back, and pushing against my body, wrested himself free. I reached for an ankle, but missed. What good would it do to drag him down with me? I would still be dead. And killing me was obviously the guy's intention. I needed to escape.

I reached for his ankle again. He kicked the side of my head and knocked my mask askew. Water leaked under the plastic. I punched at his leg, but punching through water was useless. I needed to get my hand out of the water. I needed to get my head up for air.

He was stronger and pushed me deeper. Instead of

struggling, I paddled my arms to move a little deeper, the lack of resistance catching him off guard. Bobbing to the surface beside him, I pulled my mask off and gasped for breath.

Using both hands and all my strength, I launched the hard plastic snorkel tube into his nose, just like people said you should do to a shark.

His hands flew to his nose and I splashed through the water, trying to put myself in the line of vision of the few people on the beach. My torso screamed in pain.

He swam after me.

"Help!" I shrieked. I waved my hands frantically. "¡*Ayudame!*"

I curled into a ball so there would be less to grab and frantically twisted my braid away from him. His hand snagged my bathing suit. Blood drizzled from his nose. I kicked for the bull's eye, but my heel landed on his cheek. The water cushioned the full force of my attack. As I started to yell for help again, warm salt water gushed into my throat. I stabbed blindly with the snorkel.

Suddenly I bounced to the surface, again. People on the beach were staring. My attacker was swimming away to his boat. Panting, I treaded water.

The strong, slender figure pulled himself into his boat. No name scrolled across the transom, but it had red trim and a big, shiny Yamaha engine perched on the stern. I noted with satisfaction that he swiped under his nose as he started his engine. Then he roared away.

I floated back to shore, mask in hand, kicking with rubbery legs.

CHAPTER 22

Coyote Gee thought of the little girl and prayed she was quick. Kids were great catches for drug smugglers, with nimble fingers for cutting and bagging, vulnerable, easy to chain to a chair, less likely to fight or escape. Slave labor. And little girls, well. . . .

"Kids," the white voice scoffed. "I can't stand their sorry-ass whining. They've all scattered by now, anyway."

Coyote Gee stopped working at the tangled mess of tape around the young man's wrists and ripped the duct tape from his ankles.

Outside, the boots stopped. The Mexican spoke. "Check out this van, though." It sounded like: "Sheck out thees ban, dough." A fist rapped on the metal. "All set up to smuggle. Cool."

Coyote Gee huddled against his shaking prisoner and bit at the duct tape around his wrists. If he could free his prisoner, it would be two against two. The plane had sounded small. They probably did not have anyone else. Even two was a surprising waste of space.

One man laughed, deep-throated and pleased. "Keys." The Mexican voice. "Those wetbacks ran off in a hurry," he said in Spanish.

"Shut your mouth," the white man growled in Spanish, opening the door of the van and climbing behind the wheel.

Coyote Gee chewed a tiny gash in the tape. Grabbing on either side, he used all his strength and pulled.

The rip resounded in his ears and echoed against the

metal walls like a volcanic explosion. The white man whirled, knocking off his cowboy hat. A gleaming pistol pointed at the noise.

Coyote Gee reached up and yanked open the side door.

"Don't shoot 'em in here," the other man screamed.

Coyote Gee dove into the sand. It felt almost as bad as the time he'd landed on the freeway. His collarbone shot bolts of pain.

A couple hundred pounds landed on top of him and panted in his ear. Coyote Gee smelled the warm earth and the fresh desert air and the rancid odor of the man who had pinned him. The gun clicked and cold metal pressed to his temple.

For his last breath, he concentrated on the fragrance of the desert.

CHAPTER 23

The professor supplied me with Band-Aids for my coral cut, but I had not been able to communicate the idea of hydrogen peroxide. Even after I showered away the salt water, the slice above my ankle stung like unrequited love. I felt restless. The trek back to the hotel had not calmed my adrenal gland. I was pumped up. I wanted to go into town and see if I spotted a young guy with a swollen nose. My imagination rendered up a few thousand tortures for him, which included stabbing him in the neck with a fork, and kicking him behind the knee so he fell onto the sidewalk and I could use his back as a trampoline. Were these normal responses, or in addition to hot flashes, had menopause blessed me with anger issues?

My fingers trembled as I dressed. I coughed, my chest sore from swallowing water and fighting for air with an already bruised rib. Residual pepper spray burned with each cough. I tested the purple splotch on my rib cage. Yup. It hurt. It promised eventually to color a swatch as large as an orange. I looked forward to it—outward evidence of my vacation from hell, my merit badge for stupidity. Why did I go sticking my nose in where it didn't belong? Somehow these events had to be connected. The guy in the water didn't attack me for no reason. I flopped back on the bed and burped up salt water. When I replayed my near drowning, my body shook so hard the mattress vibrated like a cheap by-the-hour hotel love nest.

I pulled myself up and bent over carefully to put on my flip-flops. I tried to re-braid my hair, but I could not control my arms. The man had meant to kill me. Could have killed me.

Almost killed me. Jesus.

As I had neared the beach, awkwardly, still holding the mask, my arms feeling like bricks, a few people on the sand had gawked, but none of them had jumped in to save me. They had stared shyly and uncertainly as I stumbled from the water.

A matronly woman asked me if I was okay. I told her in Spanish that I was. She asked me what happened. I started to explain and then sat on the sand, defeated, batting her away in frustration, unable to think of the word for drown.

When the other two snorkelers glided up to the beach, I asked them if they were going back to La Ropa Beach and if I could walk with them.

They were Canadians, graying but spry, and said "Of course" almost in unison. They didn't press me for information, but as we clambered over the rocks, I told the story in broad strokes.

"Why on earth did this fellow try to drown you?" the woman exclaimed.

"Good question," I replied.

Now, in my hotel room, I gave up trying to braid my heavy hair and hitched it into a messy, wet ponytail. I considered the possibilities: the guy was crazy, or his attempt to kill me had a motive, something to do with Lalo or with my search for my father.

I wished I had my Colt. I wished I were home. I wished I were in a country where I could trust the police.

Walking to town might wear off my hyped anxiety. In spite of the glaring sun and the other fatigued, sunburnt tourists along the path, my head swiveled vigilantly for any sign of danger, and I covered the ground to town in record time.

I strode along the promenade, my heart still pounding from my near-death experience, staring like a mad woman at all the passing young, slim Mexican males. Even as I knew the idea I might run into my attacker was obsessive, perhaps insane, I couldn't stop myself.

"Hey there," a voice called.

I spun around. Vibrant red and orange and purple woven wool rugs accented a green stucco wall.

"Behind the rhododendron." The *sotto voce* whisper was worthy of a smoking, trench-coated figure from a noir film.

I peeked behind the potted plants that separated a restaurant from the sidewalk.

"Hello there," Mark Escalante gaily greeted me. He pulled off his Bucci's as though I might not recognize him otherwise. He looked fresh and showered, not like a man who had spent the night in a Mexican jail.

I, on the other hand, reeked of nervous sweat and had all the sex appeal of a dead fish. "How did you get out?"

"My lawyer arrived about noon. It didn't take him long," he gloated. He raised a beer to his lips. "Damn, this tastes good."

I sat across from him. He'd exchanged his tourist disguise for a form-fitting black muscle shirt. "I'm surprised they didn't ask you to leave the country."

"Oh, believe me, they did. However, you may have noticed this little airport doesn't exactly have flights every hour. And I need something where I can connect to Arizona."

"Arizona?"

The waiter approached and I ordered a beer.

"Home," he explained. "Tucson. Don't tell me you thought I was from Northern California." He said it like one of those people who regards the area as a cesspool of liberalism.

My face, as usual, must have been as loose-lipped as a gossip column because he continued, "I was in California to take care of some business and to connect with Margy, my videographer."

"Videographer?" I asked snidely.

He stared; I flushed. I had wondered how his lawyer arrived so promptly. Clearly Margy contacted him as soon as Mark had been hauled off to jail.

My beer arrived with a small plate of sliced limes. I took

a swig and my rib reminded me it wasn't happy. I ravenously bit into a lime. What did he mean by *connect*? "So you two work together?"

His face hardened into a none-of-your-business mask.

"I'm surprised the police cared about your flight's destination."

"They didn't. If it were up to them, I'd probably be on a flight to Atlanta as we speak." He smirked again and nursed his beer. "But that's why I have a lawyer who specializes in international law. I'm not exactly an illegal alien they can deport any old place. Notice, though, that they still have a couple of goons watching me." He pulled aside broad rhododendron leaves and nodded at two police officers lounging on the dark brown rim of a large orange planter. The older one was lighting a cigarette, the younger one was admiring the backside of a passing girl.

"I'm sorry my . . . friend . . . couldn't spring you."

"Oh, yeah, your friend," he chuckled. "Geraldo Sabala, with an s."

I frowned. His reaction seemed bizarre. Was he showing off his memory, his attentiveness to detail?

"That's okay," he continued. "If he had sprung me, my lawyer would have come all the way down here for nothing."

"You seem happy. I guess everything's going as planned. Lalo is going to be extradited?" I chewed a second lime slice.

"At the moment I think so."

"Well, be on guard," I said.

He raised an inquiring eyebrow.

Maybe it was the solid look of Mark's chest muscles, the cleft visible under the black cotton. Maybe it was the intimacy of having gone to jail together. Maybe it was my own pent-up emotions of feeling alone and vulnerable. Whatever the reason, I spilled my guts—from renting the snorkel on La Ropa Beach to using it as a weapon against my assailant.

Mark listened sympathetically, but when I had finished he smiled. "So you've hoofed it to town to work your gumshoe magic and track down a guy with a swollen nose?"

"Actually, I've come to town to thank. . . ."

"The Canadians?"

"No," I said annoyed. "They're staying in La Ropa Beach."

"Ah, yes, your friend. The one with the get-out-of-jail-free card." He drained his beer.

I let the sarcasm slide. After my time with David Shapiro, I had grown impervious to sarcasm. I gnawed on a slice of lime.

"Want some beer with that?"

I glowered, but took a careful sip. Anger flared in me. My attacker had made it so I couldn't even enjoy a beer.

"I imagine the guy was one of Lalo's friends," Mark said. "That's one thing about tracking guys into Mexico, you can pretty much count on them going where they have friends and family. Most of Lalo's family is in Mexico City. Tourism industry. But his father's side originated over here. Lalo would have been smarter disappearing into Mexico City, but fortunately for me, he's not exactly a mastermind." Mark Escalante stretched both of his muscular arms overhead, as happy and smug as a cat in the sun. Even though his eyes looked tired from the night in jail, they glowed with dollar signs cha-chinging at the end of his journey. He relaxed his arms and rolled his neck. "I love stupid criminals. California boy that he is, Lalo couldn't resist the sun and surf. He's what Old Timers like you and me call a Good Time Charley."

"Old Timers?" I felt flattered that he included me among the experienced, but injured that he regarded me as old.

He grinned with his dimples. "You're right. 'Old' has no place in a sentence addressed to you."

His line could not have seemed more canned, and yet I smiled back. In my book, 'You're right' ranked up there with being called smart. I couldn't believe I was flirting. Why didn't I just bat my eyelashes at him? Hadn't I decided last night that I had lost all attraction? Of course, last night we had been in jail, and Mr. America himself would not have fared well in those circumstances. Sometimes it seemed to me that finding a boy-friend had more to do with being in the right time and place than with meeting a soul mate.

"You don't have to worry about Lalo's little punk friend going for me," Mark continued.

"I wasn't." Even if my attacker meant to avenge Lalo's arrest, surely he would think twice about going for Mark Escalante. Mark would snap the kid in half like a pretzel.

"Did this guy seem like he'd lived in the United States?"

"For crying out loud!" I was almost as shocked to hear my mother's words emanating from my mouth as I was at Mark's question. What had happened to my flirting? "The guy was trying to drown me. I didn't exactly notice if he acted like an American. It's not like he was wearing clothes and we had a conversation."

He smiled at the outburst. "I have two thugs in uniform dogging my every move," he said. "Let me escort you around. You'll have built-in armed body guards."

"Like you care about my life," I snapped. Success had put him in a jolly mood, but I was cranky and stiff from sleeping on a wooden bench. My torso was black and blue, and the coral cut on my ankle stung. I looked like shit. And I'd responded to a perfunctory line that contained not an iota of sincerity from a man with questionable traits in a shady business. Who no longer seemed to be flirting.

Still, why was I busting his balls? A year ago I would have described myself as fairly calm. Now I felt like I was thirteen again—uncontrolled, combustible.

Mark Escalante remained unscathed. When I finished my beer, he motioned for the waiter, paid my bill and stood, as though the matter had been decided.

As we moved down the *paseo*, the two policemen fol-lowed conspicuously fifty feet behind us. They both wore dark blue baseball caps with *Policia* stenciled in bright yellow over the brim. The younger one sported a mustache and carried a submachine gun, the ammo clipped to the opposite side of his belt. The older one carried a more modest weapon, but had the walkie-talkie clipped to his belt. Since the police had been responsible for my night in hell, their presence did little to make me feel safe.

"Look," I told Mark, "I'm going up to talk to my friend. I don't really want this tag team."

"I'll hang out on the sidewalk and eat pizza."

"No. If you do that, my friend will have to bake it."

"I'll just have a beer."

"Didn't you just have one?"

"The operative word there, Carol, is one. What else am I going to do with these goons following me?"

I sighed. I didn't really have any control over where Mark Escalante chose to sit and drink a beer. He'd returned to his contentious self. Flirting wasn't Mark Escalante's natural tendency any more than it was mine.

When we reached La Pizza, he parked himself. The girl's pink flip-flops slapped across the concrete to his outdoor table. I entered the dark, steamy, blissfully empty interior.

No one was there. Not even behind the counter.

The little girl trotted back into the room.

"*¿Dónde está su papá?*"

"Today he is not working," she told me in Spanish, flipping up the entranceway in the counter and disappearing into a back room.

A woman emerged, plump and pleasant looking. Like the girl, she wore a yellow apron. She pushed back hair that curled to her shoulders.

When I introduced myself, she responded by pointing at herself and saying, "Ana Sabala." She smiled shyly at me, revealing gold dental work around her teeth.

"Geraldo's wife?" I asked in Spanish.

"*Sí.*"

I started to explain who I was, but she nodded vigorously

and said, "*Sí. Sí. Claro. La Americana.*"

The girl flipped back the counter with one hand, the other hand holding aloft a platter crowned with a cold beer and plate of lime wedges.

The mother hissed at her and jerked her head. The girl slid the platter on to the counter. Ana Sabala excused herself, lifted the platter and glided out of the room to serve Mark Escalante.

The girl ducked shyly under the counter and fled into the back.

What was that all about?

I peered out the doorway. Mark spoke to Ana, showing off his dimples. Ana smiled back. I felt annoyed, but then how could Mark know I wanted to talk to this woman. The two policemen rested against the stucco seawall. The older enjoyed another cigarette. The younger man watched two girls pass, walking arm in arm. The girls were about fifteen and wore polo tops and the skirts of schoolgirls. The young officer's head, then neck, and eventually his whole torso turned to admire the swishing maroon pleats.

It dawned on me why Ana had served Mark. Eighteen was the legal drinking age in Mexico, and probably the legal serving age as well. Even though just that morning I'd seen a boy of about six lugging home a large plastic bag of groceries, a *caguama* of beer clasped against his chest, a person didn't want to violate the law right in front of *La Policía*. Clearly Ana didn't miss much.

She talked to Mark, gesticulating with the empty platter, flashing her glittering teeth. In the back, the girl busily whacked away at something.

I was getting nothing done fast.

I walked out into the dazzling sun. Ana's laugh sparkled like the light on the ocean.

Ana blushed, whether from being caught mid-flirt or for deserting me, I didn't know. She fell silent.

"Ana was just telling me she knows a guy with a bloody

nose," Mark remarked casually.

Even though I felt weak, I remained standing. Away from the table. Whenever I got near Mark, my life became a run-away train. Why was he tangling himself in my concerns? I couldn't tell if he liked me or if he had another ulterior motive or maybe a confusing mix of the two.

Ana's dark eyes inspected me, and then shifted back to Mark. A white couple sat down at a nearby table, and looking relieved, she excused herself.

"I didn't come down here to get revenge," I hissed.

"You didn't?" he asked flatly. "My mistake."

The muggy heat sapped my energy. I felt faint, almost dizzy. I sagged into a chair of a neighboring table. I relived the morning, the weight pushing me under, the salt water rushing into my mouth, my arm thrusting the snorkel. My arm twitched and jerked as though I were in the moment. I hacked, and pounded my chest as though to expel liquid from my lungs.

Mark handed me a lime wedge. "Suck on this."

I bit into the bitterness. Tears sprang to my eyes. What would it have been like to inhale a little more water, to slip away, to bob lifelessly on the surface? What had my mother's final moments been like? Had she been aware of the end, of the last breath, of passing into darkness, into non-existence?

CHAPTER 24

I stood shakily and followed Ana back into the little restaurant. She ducked under the counter and called to her daughter.

"I want to talk to Geraldo," I said.

She glanced away. "He's not here."

"*Claro*," I said, struggling to keep my voice even. Before the near fainting spell, the woman had already regarded me as a marginal character. *La Americana*, indeed. *La Americana Loca,* the crazy American, was more like it.

The little girl appeared. The mom stood behind her and placed both of her hands on the girl's shoulders, as though she were a human shield.

I stared at the two of them connected, mother and daughter. Ruthless self-pity plunged an ice pick into my heart. I had no one——no one to grasp my shoulder, no shoulders to grasp.

And now the two of them, together, watched *La Americana Loca* tear up some more. The girl popped under the hinged counter and led me to a table.

The mother folded the counter back and followed. She ordered the little girl to take a Coke and lemonade to the new customers.

Ana sat next to me. "You think Geraldo is your brother," she said in Spanish.

"Yes." I swiped at the tears and felt foolish. I had never, ever considered myself a woman who resorted to crying to get things, and yet here, I thought sarcastically, it worked so well. Heat rose to my face. Oh, Jesus, couldn't life cut me a break?

In a moment my face would look like a soggy doughnut. "I just want to ask him about his father. Where is he? What does he do? What does he look like now?"

Ana smiled sympathetically. "Geraldo does not speak much of his father."

"Why?" I fanned myself with an ineffectual hand. I had forgotten to bring Mark's sock.

Her daughter paraded through La Pizza holding a tray of ice-cold drinks above her forehead. She delivered them to the two new customers. Mark had disappeared. I felt disappointed, but relieved. I wouldn't have any back up, but I wouldn't have anyone trying to direct my course of action, either.

Ana delivered her considered response to my question. "Perhaps he is ashamed."

"Why ashamed?" Who was this man, my possible father, that no one wanted to claim?

"He is a *pollero*. We have not heard from him in a long time."

"A *pollero*?" The word sounded like some sort of chicken farmer.

"A *coyote*."

A *coyote*. This was a word with a connotation like pirate. No, not as romantized—only as sneaky, sly, and greedy. More like a slave trader, trafficking in humans.

"Isn't he old for that kind of work?"

Ana shrugged. "Retirement is for rich Americans."

"I need to talk to Geraldo," I implored. I squeezed my eyes to make more tears.

Alligator tears or real, they did the job.

"We live in Almacén, over the Golden Gate Bridge," Ana said. She rattled off directions.

I picked up the bottom of my tee shirt and wiped my face.

The Golden Gate Bridge was an old rickety wooden structure. As I hesitated, a man selling unshelled peanuts from a gunnysack stared at me quizzically. Some adventure travelers paid top dollar to traipse over such quaint bridges, but one near-death experience per vacation was my limit. The old man gestured toward his sack. Did I want some peanuts?

"No, *gracias.*"

The bridge spanned about 100 yards over a marina. I wondered how far one had to walk inland to circumnavigate the water, far enough to be hiking out by the forested hills where the professor told me endangered cougars roamed? Or would I simply be pushed into a labyrinth of unfamiliar streets?

I took a tentative step onto the bridge. It swayed. I grabbed a pole for support. Then I saw the boat leaving the municipal pier—small and white with red trim. There must have been a dozen white boats with red trim, but how many had engines that sparkled and glinted in the sun?

I squinted, but I couldn't make out the man, much less whether he had a swollen nose. Could he identify me, alone on the bridge? Certainly my looking like a *güera* gave him a huge advantage. Add to that my distinctive mane of auburn hair.

I ran, the bridge bobbing and shaking. I wanted a big lead if my assailant decided to return to the pier to pursue me. Fortunately I was headed to an area called La Noria, away from the Bay of Zihuatanejo.

Safely across the bridge, I took a deep breath, then hurried along the cobble-stoned road, my flip-flops spitting up bits of gravel. If I had known where this outing would take me, I would have worn my Teva sandals. This was not an area that had been spiffed up for tourists. Garbage overflowed from cans and stray cats rummaged on top the heap, stirring the stench of rotted fish. Wrought iron fences topped with chicken wire guarded the run-down stores to my left. Rebar protruded from the tops and fronts of the stucco buildings, so they had a construct-now-finish-*mañana* look.

Why had the guy tried to drown me? Killing me seemed extreme to avenge a friend's arrest. I thought of Mark's immediate question about whether the guy acted like an American. I had to hand it to Mark; as a more experienced hound dog, he cut right to the chase. If my attacker had lived in the United States, maybe he was running from the law, too. Maybe he had helped Lalo with the double homicide. Maybe there was some bounty to be made. If the guy had spotted me, would he want to finish the job he'd started that morning? I didn't want to dawdle and find out.

As I scuttled along, dust infiltrated my Band-Aid and bit into the coral cut. My chest burned from pepper spray mist and a near drowning. I coughed. The coughing turned to hacking. Propping myself with one hand against an Amate tree, I crossed my legs tight so I wouldn't pee in my shorts. Rubbing my chest with my free hand, I tried to soothe it. When my body reached its fill of coughing, I felt exhausted.

There were a few old men playing cards in front of one of the dim, unlit stores, but otherwise the road was empty. Of course. It was siesta time. Only a loony strolled about in the afternoon sun.

I rested for a moment against the tree. The professor had one of these fig trees in his garden. I had remarked on its beauty, smiled at the name *amate*, which meant "love yourself."

"It's also called the *matapalo*," the professor had explained.

Stick killer. Lovely.

"You see, at first it surrounds the closest tree like it's hugging it," the professor continued, "but then it strangles it."

Just like my relationships—my overly protective former husband Chad, and the bossy, domineering on-hold boyfriend David. Even the push/pull relationship with my mom had felt suffocating.

I cast myself from the bark and focused on boats. The guy didn't need to return to the pier to pursue me. To my right was a dirt-packed park strewn with garbage and beyond the marina continued inland.

With my flip-flops and aching chest, I couldn't quite run, but I moved quickly up the road, the world bright, hot, and so silent I could hear plants move.

The weeds rustled and I jumped. The narrow path of a lizard or a snake swished through the growth. I glanced back over my shoulder. A woman and her daughter emerged from one of the stores, but headed toward the bridge. I was alone. I took the second left, a street of shacks mixed with modest, crumbling stucco houses, sporting wrought iron bars on the windows or wrought iron fences running from ground to rooftop. Ana had not bothered with an address. A blue house on the right.

The street was concrete and steep. I passed a graceful tamarind tree drooping long, dark pods, a rusted out Pontiac muscle car, and a coop of roosters.

A rock popped. I spun around. No one. But lizards and snakes didn't make rocks crunch. I tore up the road, cursing my flip-flops, twisting to glance behind me, and then turning my head left and right, even though Ana had said right, looking for blue, blue, blue.

I spotted blue and sprinted. It was on the left, but I didn't care. I unlatched the gate and entered a small, tidy patio shaded by a tree and ornamented by large clay pots of hibiscus and coleus.

I pounded on the door. The varnish was long gone and the wood was splintering. A dog yipped. I looked down the deserted street and felt foolish. I knew this was the wrong door. As I rubbed my aching chest and ribs, the door dragged open and a wizened old lady stared at the apparition before her.

"*Bueños dias,*" I managed.

The traditional garb one saw in gift stores—a white cotton dress richly embroidered—hung from her frame. She used one spindly leg to block the path of a raging Chihuahua. He barked like he smelled the blood of my coral wound.

"*Bueños dias,*" I tried again. My heart settled into a natural rhythm. If my attacker lunged through the gate, I could push aside this old lady and slam the door. The Chihuahua might have my ankle for lunch, but at least I'd be alive.

With a knobby finger the woman pointed to her ear.

Deaf. Just my luck.

"Geraldo Sabala!" I shouted, in case she wasn't completely deaf.

She shook her head, but I didn't know if that meant she couldn't hear or if Geraldo Sabala was meaningless gibberish to her.

She pointed to her mouth, the lip-less, collapsed hole of an old person without dentures. She indicated a caned patio chair and closed the door.

An unreasonable panic seized me. I wanted to charge the door like a raiding police officer.

I peered into the street. If my assailant was tracking me, he was showing restraint and stealth. I stood mired in indecision. Did I sit on the inviting worn leather seat and wait for this old lady who couldn't protect me other than by bearing witness? Did I continue up the street to find Geraldo's house? What were the chances the guy on the boat was "the guy" and had spotted me and followed me? Did waiting here protect me or provide him time to catch me?

I sat on the chair under a strange tree. Green fruit the size of baseballs grew directly out of the trunk and branches.

When I brought my gaze down, he was standing at the gate, calmly, wearing the same black swim trunks. His chest was bare, but he wore athletic shoes with no socks. White adhesive tape bridged his nose. He lifted the latch and I sprang from my seat and pushed at the heavy door. It gave way and I tumbled into the little old lady. I grunted in surprise.

The Chihuahua danced at my feet baring its teeth. I apologized in Spanish and then remembered she couldn't hear. The woman peered into the yard with rheumy eyes. Could she see any better than she could hear?

"¡*Mátele*!" she growled.

Kill her! Holy shit. Was she allies with my attacker or just frightened by my craziness?

I jumped out the door. His strong, wiry body crouched,

ready to pounce, in the small area between me and the gate. The wrought iron fence was too high to clear even with my former volleyball legs. I did what my cat Lola would do. I went for the tree. I sprang for the lowest branch and pulled myself into its gnarled web in time to feel, more than see, a white, meaty blur rush by. I plucked one of the fruit to use as a weapon, but the young man bolted for the gate. Before he could reach it, a white pit bull locked itself to his bare calf.

The man shrieked.

"¡*Pare!*" the woman commanded and the dog released its prize.

Even from the tree, I could see the ring of bleeding teeth marks.

She aimed an arthritic finger at the gate and screamed at the young man to get out. Overkill, since the slobbering beast stood ready to rip into his other leg.

He limped to the outside of the chipped black fence and then bent to examine his wound. He swore, using every bad word in Spanish I had ever learned.

They didn't faze the tiny lady, who couldn't hear them. She yelled at him some more, not all of which I understood, but I caught the gist: that if he ever came on her property again, she would kill him.

Mátale.

That was the trouble with Spanish; the "le" could mean him or her.

The guy hobbled down the road.

The woman walked to the fence and shouted him along. She picked up a clod of earth and heaved it at him for good measure. The action would have been ridiculous without the dog at her side. The pit bull quivered with muscle, a truly ugly creature with pink-rimmed eyes and mouth. She patted the dog. "Chato, Chato," she murmured affectionately.

"Is it safe to get down?" I called, even though she was stone deaf.

Surprisingly she turned and motioned me down. She laughed when she saw the fruit in my hand. "¿*Una arma?*" she asked loudly. A weapon?

She launched into an explanation of the tree, called a *cirián*, at a volume that suggested I shared her deafness. The gourd could be used on bruises, she said, pointing at the purplish area around the dirty Band-Aid on my ankle. The pulp was also good for coughs, she added.

Hmmm. I kept the fruit in my hand.

"Do you know that guy?" I shouted in Spanish.

She pointed to her ear and smiled apologetically.

I made the motion of writing. She nodded and turned to her house.

I cast a glance at the pit bull and she whistled for him to follow. She did not invite me into the house, so I stood nervously on the patio. What would I do when I had to leave the woman's protection? Hopefully the guy had been frightened away, had gone off somewhere to treat the dog bite. Or if he had stayed, I hoped he was too incapacitated to chase me. But what if he ambushed me? What if he had his own weapon, something better than a green gourd?

The tiny woman returned with a stub of pencil with no eraser, a prison pencil. It had been sharpened with a knife, the lead flat-edged. For paper she supplied the back of a grocery receipt.

I gestured for her to have the seat, but she shook her head vigorously, indicating that I, the company, should sit. I could not take the chair and have the old woman stand. I didn't see any other chair and I wondered if the woman were too poor to afford another, or if no one visited her, or if the *feng shui* of one chair suited her. I sat on the dusty brick patio and placed the strange fruit beside me.

Seeing that I was stubborn, the woman settled into the chair. So stubborn I refused to be born, my mom used to say. Apparently my brother Donald had more or less popped out of her, and she'd been duped into thinking childbirth was not such a big deal. Then she had me.

I started to write on the paper, creating bumpy letters against the brick surface.

The old woman shook her head and explained in her loud, crackly voice that she could not read cursive. While in the house, she'd inserted dentures; the teeth looked too big for her mouth.

In Spanish I printed: Do you know that guy?

I didn't have to hold the paper very close to her before she issued a biting string of words: troublemaker, little devil, criminal. "*Mamas a dos tetas.*"

This literally meant he sucked on two tits, but I supposed it was idiomatic: some sort of double dealer?

Clearly, though her eyes were cloudy with cataracts, she could see fairly well. Her harsh bluntness reminded me of my mother. I missed that voice—tough, practical, familiar.

How do you know him? I penciled.

"¡*Mi vecino!*" she shouted as though it were perfectly obvious. Her neighbor.

Like Santa Cruz, Zihuatanejo might have outgrown an identity as a sleepy coastal fishing village, but it still offered small-town encounters.

What is his name?

"Hugo. Hugo Morales." She followed this with a vituperative speech that I could only half follow, but I gathered Hugo had been the neighborhood thief. His poor mother, on the other hand, was a lovely woman and his father a saint, and all the other children in the family, Maria, and Liliana, and Perla, and Gustavo, the list seemed endless, all church members of the community. How did this happen to good, god-loving people?

I wanted to ask her dozens of questions about the guy who had tried to kill me, but the receipt didn't allow much more space.

I placed the small paper on the patio. Do you know Geraldo Sabala?

CHAPTER 25

The man on top of him did not pull the trigger. Coyote Gee was alive to hear the robber from the van thump onto the road. The cowboy, the gringo, pounded after him, but the robber was young and fast.

The crack split the desert air. Then another and another and another. The cowboy was firing blindly into the moonless darkness. But one of the bullets must have hit home because there was the thump and surprised grunt of a wounded animal.

The man on top of Coyote Gee swore in Spanish. "Fucking stupid idiot white fucker." He muttered, "Tells me to keep my mouth shut and then fires his gun." His weight released slightly and Coyote Gee bucked and twisted and pitched the man to the ground.

Coyote Gee then ran, hunched over and ready to be shot. He zigzagged to make himself a more difficult target. The sand sucked at his shoes and they felt like sacks of grain. His pants swished through the brush and the cursing man behind him told him to stop and he almost laughed at the ridiculous command.

The cowboy charged toward them from the side and fired his gun. A coyote yammered and the stars pulsed with his beating heart.

Then another blast, the muzzle flash from the corner of his eye, and the crunch of his skull, faster than he could think *I'm dead.*

CHAPTER 26

The old woman nodded vigorously. *Otro vecino. Un buen hombre.* Another neighbor. A good man. She rattled on that he had painted the front of her house with his leftover paint. She loved the color. *Azul.*

I didn't want to appear impatient. The woman and her pit bull had just saved my life.

I returned the receipt to the bricks and found a space to print: Where?

"Just up the street. A blue house, like mine," she shouted proudly.

There were so many questions I wanted to ask her: What's your name? Could I borrow your pit bull? How did you know I was at the door?

But I was out of space.

I picked up the green gourd, pointed at it and pointed at me.

The old woman cackled and indicated the tree. Did I want more?

I shook my head and told her thanks, hoping she might read my lips.

She watched me stand and fell silent.

"*Mucho gusto en conocerle,*" I said. A pleasure to meet you. I extended a hand.

She stood. The total of her came up to my chest. Her wrinkles, her shoulders, everything seemed to slump, but she gripped my hand with surprising strength. "Magdalena de la Cruz." She proudly patted her chest.

I smiled.

She released my hand and began a loud speech of farewell, a pleasure to meet you, thank you, and what a lovely young woman, and go with God. . . .

At the gate, I looked nervously both ways.

"Do you want to take Chato?" she asked. She didn't wait for an answer but rather stuck her fingers in her mouth and whistled.

The meaty rush came from the back of the house and screeched to a halt at her leg.

The hairs on my neck prickled. If I touched the dog, it might tear my hand off.

The woman bent down and had a serious conversation with the animal. She spoke slowly and at a slightly reduced volume, as if to a child, as she explained to Chato that he was supposed to guard me.

I didn't know what to say, not that it mattered, since the woman couldn't hear me. I shook my head, but the woman opened the gate and the dog walked proudly into the street. The red-rimmed eyes looked expectantly back at me as though it had understood every word the woman had said.

"He is very friendly," the old woman assured me.

It didn't look like any leash was about to materialize.

I passed through the gate. "Hello, Chato."

It wagged its stub of tail.

I strolled down the street with the killing machine at my side.

Geraldo Sabala's house was a bigger place, painted blue all the way around, or at least on the front and the side that I could see, with vibrant orange trim. He didn't have any fence, but he had black wrought iron bars over his windows. His small concrete patio was surrounded by trees. In the shade of a banana tree, in front of the house, Geraldo Sabala squatted by the open engine compartment of an ancient tan Volkswagen bug.

He glanced up, registering no surprise, and said hello to me in English. His greeting to the dog was much more enthusiastic. The pit bull waggled its hips toward Geraldo who patted him and scratched his ears until the dog licked his face.

Glancing over my shoulder, I squatted beside him and set down my fruit. The street resonated with the quiet of siesta time. There was no sign of Hugo Morales or anyone else. "What's wrong with your car?"

"It runs like this." He illustrated jerking with his hand. In a grease-stained undershirt, Geraldo looked much more Americanized even though he still wore brown polyester pants. For a married, family man, he sported good definition across the chest and down his arms.

Peering into the engine compartment, caked with old grease, I wondered how one said "fuel filter," "spark plugs" or "distributor cap" in Spanish? As soon as I thought I had a handle on the language, I realized I could fill the universe with things I didn't know.

However, I knew a bit about the engine and electrical system in front of me since I drove a '66 Karmann Ghia, and Ghias and bugs shared the same guts from 1956 until well into the 70's. Living on a baker's salary, I had learned to do my own tune-ups and small repairs. My poor Ghia sat forlornly now at the San Francisco Airport in the rain and fog. Cars, like people, were made to move; they liked warm oil flowing, pistons cranking, and tires turning. They did not like to sit, oil crusting and air leaking.

Faced with my lack of vocabulary, I touched the fuel filter and asked in Spanish, "Have you changed this recently?"

Geraldo shook his head and said in English, "The fuel filter is sort of new."

I had forgotten how well he spoke English. Pathetic tools littered the dirt. If he did his own mechanical work, he operated in a primitive way. I didn't spot any spark plug socket wrench.

He scratched under a nostril and smeared oil into his overgrown mustache. "That guy you were with in jail smelled like a cop."

I shrugged and kept my eyes on the grimy engine compartment. The gray fan belt appeared taut. "I barely met the guy on the plane." Two could play at the game of pretend casual conversation. "People thought we were together; it was one of those wrong-place-at-the-wrong-time kind of things." I wiggled the spark plug wires to see if any were loose, and wondered about the quality of the gas in Mexico. That could make a car run ragged, too.

The dog rested on its haunches by Geraldo and they both watched me with wrinkled foreheads.

"So you aren't any kind of law enforcement?"

"I'm just a gal searching for her father." Even with both of them at my side, I took another look up and down the street before picking up a greasy rag. I wrapped a clean spot around my finger, and wiped off the distributor cap, standing to see the back of it.

"Here is your problem." Happily, I could say that perfectly in Spanish.

Geraldo rose, eyebrows lifted in disbelief. He followed my finger. "*Una raja.*"

I didn't know this word either, but I assumed he had seen the hairline fissure. With this heat, it was not surprising that over time the plastic had dried and cracked.

I switched back to English. "The contacts are probably corroded from the sea air." Spanish was so much more consistent, so much easier to learn than English. Yet even after years, a conversation that required particular vocabulary left me stymied.

He nodded.

Straightening up reminded me of how many aches I had. I stretched my back, and did a quick visual inspection of the silent street. I massaged my bruised rib.

Geraldo asked if I would like some water.

My mouth felt like paste and I would have loved some cold water, but not enough to risk Montezuma's Revenge.

Geraldo saw my hesitation, understood, and offered a beer. He waved me to a white plastic patio table on the other side of the banana tree. I settled on a dusty chair as Geraldo disappeared. No one in Zihuatanejo wasted precious water on grass. Geraldo's concrete patio put him a step-up from the people with dirt yards. Once upon a time the concrete had been bright orange to match the house trim.

At my feet, Chato rested his head onto his paws. I wished Hugo Morales would show up again, so I could sic the ugly critter on his other leg.

I told Chato, in Spanish, that he was a good dog. He lifted an ear to catch my words and sighed in contentment. I felt a pang of disloyalty to Lola. Bad enough that I had left her to the care of my neighbor; here I was murmuring sweet nothings to a dog.

Even though it was unnecessary, in my head I practiced the Spanish of the questions I needed to ask Geraldo. He returned, set a plate of sliced limes on the table, and handed me a cold bottle of beer, an unfamiliar type of Dos XX in a green bottle. His hands were rosy from scrubbing off grease. For a short while, we were both content to sit in the shade and swig our drinks.

I started the conversation, in Spanish, by thanking him for getting me out of jail.

He waved his hand. "*De nada*. You found the problem with my car. We're even. Besides, that is the reason we have family."

My heart surged, but then I realized he might be referring to his cousin, or whoever she was, at the jail—not me.

"I see you met Lalo's grandmother," he continued.

He smiled at my stunned surprise.

Oh my God. His smile was Donald's and I was transported instantly to a summer day drinking bottled beer on the rocks along the Eel River. Donald's dark hair was plastered to his skull. Drops of water dried on his slim brown torso. We watched his friend's body slip along under the clear water like a seal and Donald shot me that blazing smile. At that moment, I should have known. But for all my efforts to be a tough bad girl, I remained provincial and innocent. And self-absorbed, like most teenagers. I never did "get it." Donald had to come out to me.

Geraldo nodded at the pit bull wheezing at my feet. "Mrs. de la Cruz. Chato's owner. She's the grandmother of that guy you got arrested."

Of course. De la Cruz. Mark had told me that Lalo had relatives in Zihuatanejo. "Lalo, Lalo, Lalo. Doesn't this guy have a real name?"

"Eduardo." Geraldo scratched his head. "I think."

"So that's why Mrs. de la Cruz knows Hugo Morales. Lalo and Hugo are buddies."

Geraldo's face sagged. "You met Hugo Morales? Everyone in this neighborhood knows him."

We had drained our second beers by the time I finished telling Geraldo about my near drowning and my recent encounter with Hugo Morales. As I spun my story this second time, I felt calmer, but Geraldo listened sullenly, sinking in his seat, as though he were being pushed under water himself. His face turned pale.

"Excuse me," Geraldo said, "I have to see a man about a horse."

"Me, too."

He ushered me into the cool dark house and showed me to a minuscule bathroom. As soon as I exited, Geraldo zipped into the bathroom like a man on a mission.

My eyes adjusted to the dim interior. Rough white plaster walls edged terracotta tiles. The furniture was sparse, all wood with caning. A clean but rather austere look. Except for the large, garish cross over the television, which emphasized the crown of thorns and the blood dripping from Jesus, the walls stood bare.

Geraldo's urine gushed. And gushed. I returned to the patio table so he wouldn't emerge knowing that I had overheard his impressive stream of pee.

When he joined me, I finally got to the point. "Ana tells me your father is a coyote." There was nothing to be gained by pressing the idea his father might also be mine.

Geraldo grunted and picked at the foil on the neck of his beer bottle.

"She says you haven't heard from him for a while."

Geraldo kept his eyes downcast. He peeled the label with a thumbnail. His delicate scratching, the dog's contented breathing, and the rustle of the banana tree leaves emphasized the stillness around us.

"I've been to Naco," he said, almost a whisper. "Everything is deserted. The mail is stacked up. I tossed out the old food."

"He could have been arrested." My suggestion fell into the afternoon quiet. "Sometimes it takes a while before a person is processed and deported," I tried. I waited in the silence and watched him strip the bottle down to bare green glass.

"He's dead," he said.

CHAPTER 27

Geraldo sounded certain.

"But you don't have a body," I protested.

"Dead is dead," he retorted angrily. "Why do I need the body?"

That sounded like something my mother would say, so matter of fact, but there were lots of reasons to want the body: to provide closure, to give the living a place of mourning and remembrance, to make me stop my insane search, but I stuck to the most factual reason. "You need the body to know if he died of natural causes." You actually needed a body to know if he was dead at all.

His jaw set and he stared out into the dusty street. "Mexicans die in the desert every day." Bitterness bit the words.

"Do you think he died in the Mexican desert or in the United States?"

He shrugged. Dead was dead. *Where* did not matter to him either. "There's less reason for him to take off running in Mexico," he said flatly. "He would have been with his car, and they should have been able to trace his identity back to me, although you can't trust the Mexican police. Maybe one of them wanted a minivan."

"Wouldn't he have a driver's license?"

He squinted at me. "Nobody going illegally into the U.S. carries real I.D."

"Oh." I felt like an idiot.

"Of course, if for some reason he wasn't with his car, his body could be ripped up and carried off. The coyotes don't care if you are in Mexico or the United States."

It took me a second to realize he meant the animal coyotes.

"I guess Ana doesn't know about your trip to Naco."

"She knows I went," he said.

"But not what you found?" I lifted my brows.

He sighed wearily and turned toward me. "You really must think he was your dad."

"I do."

He stuck a finger into each of his beer bottles and nervously tapped them together. The dog jerked up his head at the noise, quickly discerned it was harmless, and settled back on his paws. "And you want to find him, dead or alive."

I hadn't really thought about this. Did I want to find my father if he was dead? What good would that do? I flicked back to my earlier thoughts. Closure. To end this journey. A place to deliver the pink envelope.

"Yes."

"Then maybe you could go to Arizona for me."

"Go to Arizona for you?" I echoed. So he cared about his dead father after all. I felt like bashing him on the head with a beer bottle. "He's your father for sure. Why don't you go to Arizona?"

"I can't." He popped his fingers from the bottles.

"Why?" I braced myself for a litany of lame excuses: money, work, my kid, my wife. . . .

"There's a warrant for my arrest in Arizona."

Ah so. No wonder he'd caused a blip on Mark Escalante's radar. Mark Escalante who hailed from Tuscon. Geraldo inspected his lap while I searched for words. "What did you do?"

"I suppose you think I got you out of jail because I believe you are my sister, or because I am a man with a big heart. *Pero soy un hombre con un corazón llena de pena.*" He clasped his chest with both hands, a gesture that to most Americans would seem melodramatic.

I am a man with a heart full of grief. He had switched to Spanish for the exact idea. He was a man with a heavy heart.

I thought of my father. How many things had he been unable to express to my mother? How many feelings and ideas escaped his English vocabulary? How often had his expressions seemed exaggerated and ridiculous to her? Could this be part of the reason he had never returned?

Short of murder, what could Geraldo have done to inspire this chest thumping?

Geraldo stayed quiet, but I waited him out. I peeled the loose, dirty Band-Aid from the cut on my ankle and rolled it into a ball. A faint sea breeze was beginning to penetrate the hot afternoon. The leaves of the banana tree stirred. A young boy sped down the hill on a bicycle, his little sister perched on the handlebars. Both without helmets. David, my boyfriend, would be cranking up for a rant about the stupidity of riding without helmets. He's not your boyfriend, I reminded myself.

"When I was young, I went to the States," Geraldo finally began. "I wanted to go—learn English, become a successful businessman, and all those things. Land of Opportunity, you know?" He flipped his hand as though shooing a fly. "My father helped me to cross. Set me up with a friend of his. He felt guilty about my mom."

"How did your mother die?"

"Giving birth to my sister."

"You have a sister?" I couldn't quell the excitement in my voice.

"The cord," he motioned from his belly button, "wrapped around her neck."

"Oh." I thought of a woman in Ferndale who had given birth to a stillborn baby. People kept referring to how perfect the baby was. To me, my mother remarked impatiently, "Good grief. The baby's dead. How perfect is that?"

"My mother died from bleeding. Over here. In Mexico."

I sat quietly, mulling over the parallels in our lives: my absent father, his absent mother, my recently deceased mother, his recently missing father.

He broke our shared, silent sorrow. "Anyway, over there, I got in trouble."

"What kind of trouble?"

"I started running with a crew. We called ourselves Las Cucarachas." He kept his head bowed, but smiled faintly at this memory. "We came out at night."

The cockroaches. Didn't sound like a very nice crew.

"We knew we would never reach the American Dream on minimum wage. That is no excuse, but that is the way we were feeling, like what was the use. So we broke into places. We were stealing stuff."

He stopped again, played with the beer bottles. The sea breeze stirred the smells of dust and ocean. I waited as patiently as a priest in a confessional.

"One night one of those rent-a-cops showed up. Nothing to worry about usually, but this guy was high, or something. Me and two of the Cucarachas were in the stockroom of the store. A RadioShack type of store, only private. Anyway, this cowboy came back with his gun out, shouting at us. A real idiot. A clear target for anyone with a gun."

"And one of you had a gun."

"It didn't happen like that!" Geraldo flared. "What did your jail buddy say about me?"

The red-haired impatience I had inherited from my Grandpa Turner threatened my saintly aspirations. I bit my lip to keep my mouth shut.

"It wasn't some cold-blooded murder. We must have leaned too hard on the shelf, because a box fell and this guy started shooting. Like a crazy person. We thought we were going to die. That he would kill us."

"Who shot him?"

Geraldo shook his head. "Not me. That's who."

"So you fled to Mexico and became a model citizen."

"Not exactly."

CHAPTER 28

Geraldo clinked the beer bottles. "I came back here and picked up where I left off."

"That must make it tough to be part of the Chamber of Commerce, or whatever it is you have here."

"I never got caught. We mainly ripped off tourists."

"Oh, great." I reached across the table and yanked the bottles off his fingers. I slammed them down in front of me. The dog sprang up, shook out his muscles, and awaited a command to attack.

"It's not like I'm proud of it." His eyes flicked up at me.

"Who is the *we*?"

"I developed a crew." He averted his eyes again, but smiled faintly as though he were a little proud of it. "My youngest guys were Lalo and Hugo."

In his untucked white undershirt, it wasn't hard to imagine Geraldo as a gangster. Add a few gang tats on the well-defined biceps and he would fit the profile. I stared at him and his eyes finally rose to meet mine. They were much darker than Donald's and void of his sweetness. "So that's why you sprang me from jail? Because Lalo is your creation?" *And Hugo Morales!*

"People make their own choices."

Geraldo may have seen that defense didn't play well in Peoria, because he quickly added, "I did many things to pay for my crimes."

I stuffed the little bloody ball of Band-Aid into the neck of a beer bottle. *Like paint Granny de la Cruz's house?* It wasn't enough. One of Geraldo's pals had killed someone in Arizona.

Lalo had shot his wife and her boyfriend. Hugo Morales had tried to drown me. He would have killed me if he had been able to, and the man responsible for corrupting him, leading him down the wrong path, had the nerve to sit across the table from me drinking beer and calmly listening to me recount the horror. My supposed half-brother. My eyes fell to the pit bull. ¡Mátele! It was tempting.

Geraldo made kissing noises. The dog looked at me, confused, but slowly walked to the familiar hand. Geraldo cupped the pit bull's massive jaw and scratched his neck.

Anger made me hot. Sweat popped out on my forehead. Since I now accepted that my body's thermostat was broken, I mopped myself with my shirttail. I no longer cared what this thug thought of me.

"So why is this Hugo scum following me around and trying to kill me?"

Geraldo shrugged. I visualized myself flying across the table and ringing his neck. "Hugo was with Lalo over there."

"By 'over there,' you mean in the States?"

Petting the dog, he nodded.

"Do you think he helped Lalo kill his wife?"

He lifted his shoulders and eyebrows. "They came back at the same time."

If Hugo had been involved in the double homicide, no wonder he felt threatened. He may have thought Mark Escalante and I were pursuing him as much as Lalo. I stood and the dog trotted faithfully to my side.

"So you are going?"

I felt slightly ill, like I might have eaten something bad, except I hadn't eaten anything in hours. "Yes."

He shot out of his chair and smiled broadly, that smile in the photo of my dad, the smile of my brother, the smile of David Shapiro—bright and blinding. "You will?"

I had meant that I was leaving, going back to my hotel.

"You should start in Tucson." He walked briskly toward the

door into his house. "You will need photos."

I opened my mouth to protest and then didn't. He had said photos. Plural. I wanted to see these pictures. I wanted to leave Mexico having found at least a piece of my father.

The hot flash passed, but I did not sit. I did not want to be at the same table as this guy. I leaned against the banana tree, and like Newton when the apple fell on his head, I fully understood. Mark Escalante's interest in Geraldo had nothing to do with interest in me, and everything to do with bounty. Geraldo was a wanted man, a fugitive from justice, and somewhere there was a grieving family offering a reward. Nothing on Geraldo Sabala had popped up on my Internet search, but his crime would have preceded widespread computer use. In his past, Mark Escalante may have thumbed by a photo or a sketch. Or maybe just heard the name. In his line of work, a person was wired to remember faces and names.

Geraldo returned with a small handful of photos of various sizes, which he pressed into my hand.

"I hope you don't think I have some influence over Mark Escalante," I mumbled.

The remark didn't seem to register. He hovered beside me, vibrating with excitement, looking at the photos over my shoulder.

The one on top featured a pot-bellied older man with a bushy mustache standing proudly and solemnly in front of a dark minivan. For the occasion he was dressed up in cowboy boots and a white, yoked shirt.

"That one is the most recent," Geraldo said.

The dog sighed, moved to the shade under the table, circled a few times calculating maximum comfort, and then dropped down for another wait.

The photo was a full body shot, too far from the subject to be very useful. I squinted, but couldn't see any connection between this man and the one in the photo my mother had given me.

The next photo shaved off ten years and ten pounds. The

hair became more pepper and less salt. He was sitting on a caned chair holding a little girl dressed in white ruffles and lace. Her hand was lifting toward his mustache and he was smiling brilliantly down on her. And I knew, positively, absolutely, that I had found my father. And I knew positively, absolutely, that someone else had stolen his heart.

"That's my daughter," Geraldo said proudly.

I stared at the photo and touched my father's face. "What happened here?" Even in this over-exposed, yellowish photograph, pink scar tissue clearly laced the plane of his cheek.

Geraldo sidled closer and I stepped away. "He always had that scar."

"Not always," I retorted.

"Well, my whole life," Geraldo corrected, diplomatic now that he thought we were buddies again.

"Do you know how he got it?"

Geraldo smiled. "He loved those stories of trying to cross in the old days and how he was cursed. He got caught and deported every time. That scar was from his last trip. Before he became a coyote, I mean. He tried to run up the freeway and he got hit by a car. His body skidded against the concrete. Broke his collarbone."

My anger flared again. Geraldo had known from the beginning that the man in my photo didn't need to have a scar to be his father. "Then what happened?"

"They patched him up, deported him, and he married my mother. The rest is history."

I sighed. Yes, history. My whole fatherless life. I wondered now if in all those failed attempts to cross the border, he had been trying to come back to us. It would have been riskier with each attempt. The INS did not take kindly to repeat offenders now, and back then had been the era of Operation Wetback. "It's ironic someone who couldn't get across the border became a coyote."

"He says my mother changed his luck."

The statement made me feel as though I'd been pricked all over with needles. The implication from Geraldo that my father's previous family had been bad luck didn't cause my reaction. I was used to lack of tact, growing up with my mom and working for J.J. Sloan. Perhaps Geraldo's casual and full claim to my father caused it. This surprised me. I was so used to being fatherless that, had someone asked me about it a week ago, I would have said I didn't care about not having a father. Watching my mother do everything from gardening to fixing the plumbing had made me see that a woman could take care of herself.

"He also started praying to Juan Soldado," Geraldo said.

"Juan Soldado?"

"He's a folk saint. People pray to him when they cross."

I wordlessly flipped through the remaining five pictures: dressed in a tux at Geraldo Junior's wedding, one photo with his son, two more of the wedding party (young Ana with hair piled and sprayed into place except for curled tendrils organized on each plump, radiant cheek), and then two group shots at the daughter's baptism. Even though the wedding photographs were of a better quality, the closest and best shot was the yellowing one of Geraldo senior with the girl. I handed back the others.

"So this means you're going to Arizona?" Geraldo asked eagerly.

I clucked my tongue for Chato and he rose lazily from beneath the table. "No, it doesn't mean that."

Geraldo blocked my path and extended his hand. "Give me back the photo."

I shook my head.

"That picture is of my little girl."

I sidestepped him.

"I don't have many pictures of my dad," he said.

"I only have one."

"That doesn't give you the right to that." He snatched for

the picture and I jerked it back. Chato growled.

Geraldo reached down to calm the pit bull, and the dog snarled at his fingers.

Geraldo shot upright. "This is fucked, Carol."

"You got that right." I dodged completely around his body and started down the street, my bodyguard trotting at my heels. I was impressed by Chato's ability to follow instructions; he wasn't bought off with a few loving pats.

I lost some of my cockiness after I dropped off Chato with Magdalena de la Cruz. She pantomimed that I had lost my "*arma*" and did I want another of the green fruit?

I would have liked a long conversation with the woman to learn about her relationship with her grandson Lalo, but that would have been awkward in a thousand ways, not the least of which was that I had helped her grandson to be arrested.

So instead of a slow, printed exchange, I accepted another fruit. I still had to walk back to town and the sun was rapidly plummeting into the bay. A weapon might come in handy.

CHAPTER 29

I made it to town without incident, but my empty stomach was yowling like a cat in heat. I was dusty and sweaty and didn't care. I had to find a place to eat.

The sun had set and the restaurants were beginning to fill. At El Mediterráneo, a tall flamboyant man extravagantly complimented my beautiful hair, calling it the hair of a goddess, as he guided me toward a small outside table. He could not believe that such a lovely woman as I could be dining alone. Either he was upwind or the strong aromas of fish and garlic saved me. He promoted the specials in a combination of Spanish and English, both with a twist of Italian accent. His proprietary manner bespoke owner rather than *maître d'*. I planted my green fruit weapon on the floor so it wouldn't roll off the table, but would be handy.

When I went out to eat, my years as a baker were a disadvantage. I knew too much about the restaurant business, how workers didn't wash their hands as often as they should and how blackened fish often meant fish too old for a *beurre blanc* sauce. I ordered it anyway because I loved blackened fish. How old could it be in a fishing village during tourist season?

I wondered if the Italian Romeo still thought I was a goddess after he watched me scarf my food and guzzle a beer. I ordered flan for dessert and coffee. Fishing boats rocked in the twilight and flocks of people strolled the esplanade. I felt reasonably safe here, but kept a look out for a limping guy with a taped nose. I hoped it was broken.

The flan had a serious solid texture that I enjoyed, but I

missed stout Santa Cruz coffee. Exhaustion poured into my feet and worked its way up. This cup of coffee did nothing to perk up my energy. Every movement that involved lifting or twisting shot pain along my ribs.

I didn't relish leaving the security of the restaurant, but again my work experience interfered with my dining pleasure. Restaurants depended on turning over tables, and people waited to be seated. I couldn't dally any longer over my coffee without feeling guilt. I signaled for the check while I scraped up the last little specks of flan. As a single person tying up a table, I wasn't a moneymaker, so I left a generous tip.

Locals and tourists sauntered along Paseo de Pescador enjoying the balmy night, but I looked around anxiously for Hugo Morales.

Resting on the built-in steps that banked the basketball courts, I watched a group of shirtless young men charge back and forth, playing soccer under one dim light. The sea air brushed my skin. A walk back to the hotel was tempting, but I didn't want to be one of those stupid heroines who goes off alone in the dark when someone would like to kill her.

I took Cuauhtémoc, my favorite street—cobblestoned, tree-lined and foot traffic only—the one block to Juan N. Alvarez, not to be mistaken for Juan A. or Juan B. or Juan C. Alvarez. Here a person returned to the reality of a busy tourist town. I hailed one of the ubiquitous white taxis and asked him to take me to Villa Mexicana, which everyone knew, rather than to Villas Rosa, which no one knew.

When I walked up to my hotel, the professor was sitting at his outside desk reading a newspaper under a lamp. He waved me over, greeted me and motioned for me to sit. He ran through all the appropriate *saludos*: Good evening. How are you? Did you enjoy your day? Usually I appreciated this proper, polite way, but right now I wished he would get on with it.

Finally he announced that a young man had come looking for me, that he had said I needed to return some snorkel equipment. The professor raised his gray eyebrows and glanced at me over his glasses.

"Slender guy with a thin mustache and tape on his nose?" I mimed with my Spanish in case my words were wrong.

"No tape," the professor replied, "but his nose was swollen." He mimed back at me, cupping the fingers of his right hand around his nose and bouncing them. "He had a black eye, too, and a patch on his leg." The professor gazed at me, curious about the man's beat-up appearance.

Even though I was happy to hear about the burgeoning black eye, my stomach knotted. *Hugo Morales*. He must have seen me come from Villas Rosa that morning. How clever of him to use the snorkeling ruse. The professor knew I had gone snorkeling. "What did you tell him?"

The professor laid his newspaper on the desk. "I told him you were not here."

He clasped his hands on top the desk, the thumbs nervously massaging one another. The professor was no dummy. I didn't want him and Rosa to be worried and upset, but on the other hand, I prayed that he had not been intimidated, that he had not given Hugo Morales information. "What did the guy say?"

"*Preguntó si su novio estaba aquí.*"

He asked if your boyfriend was here.

The professor cocked his head and raised his eyebrows.

I shook my head and denied the existence of any boyfriend. My face flushed that the professor would have entertained the idea of a secret man in my room. Of course, given the current situation, maybe he wished I did have a boyfriend with me.

"*Entonces, pidió el número de su habitación.*"

Then he asked for your room number.

I tucked my hands between my legs so the professor would not see them tremble. I tried to think of the Spanish for "Did you give it to him?" but my mind turned to mush.

"I told him you were not here," the professor said in his carefully enunciated Spanish, changing the inflection to suggest

I was not a hotel guest at all. "I also told him that we would never give out the room numbers of our guests."

"Thank you."

He pursed his lips. "Are you in trouble?"

I didn't know what to tell the kind old gentleman. He was shrewd. He would detect a lie from me, as he had detected the lie from Hugo Morales. "Maybe," I hedged.

"We lock the gates at eleven," he reassured me.

"That is good," I replied.

"Usually Zihuatanejo is a quiet, peaceful place," he added.

"I will leave tomorrow."

"That is not necessary."

But it was necessary. The professor had not given my room number, but Villas Rosa was a very small place. Hugo Morales would soon discover my exact location. Since I had little to do with Lalo's arrest and knew only a bit about Hugo's crimes, and wouldn't give a rat's ass about him if he hadn't tried to kill me, his pursuit of me seemed unfounded and insane. Obviously he had some misguided idea of my significance. I felt like a character in a bad horror movie where the evil killer, maimed and bloody, kept coming. It would be unfair to attract the monster into the professor and Rosa's oasis.

"I would like to pay my bill now," I said, in case I had to leave in a hurry. I longed for my Colt Detective Special. It wasn't a sexy gun, but it was a reliable point and shoot. Good enough for the likes of Hugo Morales.

When I was locked in my room, I wedged a chair under the door. I scanned the room for a weapon. I unplugged the lamp, popped off its shade, unscrewed the bulb, and wrapped the cord around the wooden base. It would be almost as good as a baseball bat if the guy didn't shoot me first.

I flopped on the bed. My underarms reeked, but I could not bring myself to strip and climb in the shower. I wished I had Chato with me.

"Sorry, Lola," I muttered. My cat, deserted at home, was stuck with an automatic feeder and visits from my crazy neighbor. How alone she must feel.

Thoughts of home led to thoughts of David Shapiro. It would be comforting to have him here now. When it came to looking out for me, he was fiercer than a pit bull.

It had been a long, long day after a near-sleepless night, but my ears pricked on high alert and sleep seemed impossible. I looked at the photo I'd stolen from Geraldo Sabala. All this trouble for a stranger. I laid the photograph on the nightstand and picked up the pink envelope from my mother. Enough was enough. I tore off the duct tape, ripping the pink envelope.

Dear Carol,

If you are reading this, I knew a little duct tape wouldn't keep you out. Well, what can I say? The acorn doesn't fall far from the oak. The tape was more to hide what I just had to look at even though it was none of my business.

This letter arrived in our mailbox, and was forwarded by the people who bought our house. They said it had not been sent through the USPO. They just found it in our mailbox with your father's name on the front. Even after all these years, I thought it must be from one of your father's old girlfriends. I should have burned it or thrown it away. Instead I opened it.

It is in Spanish and from the greeting I could tell it was not a love letter. It seems to be a thank you note.

I felt ashamed for opening it. Your father did not receive many thanks in his life. He certainly did not get any from me. So, I hope you give him this letter.

Love,
Mom

She had resealed the original letter in another envelope. That was so like my mother, knowing me completely, certain I would open the pink envelope before I found my father, and not wanting me to repeat her mistakes.

The paper trembled. My mother felt alive, speaking to me. I realized more keenly than ever before that she would never speak to me again. No more clichés. No more curt advice and brusque admonitions that masked a fierce loyalty and abiding love, a deep, mute tenderness.

CHAPTER 30

A noise woke me. In my shorts and tee shirt, I was lying on top of an unfamiliar flowered bedspread. Flip-flops dangled from my feet, which hung off the side of the bed.

Moonlight revealed all the objects in the room, the chest of drawers, the desk and chair, the small, gleaming refrigerator. Everything was a green-tinged black and white. The height of the moon and the absolute silence proclaimed the witching hour.

I lay still and listened for the noise. Cha-chunk. I didn't move. In the Spartan room there was nowhere anyone could lie in wait for me. Except maybe under the bed. Adrenaline squirted through my body even as I told myself that this idea was utter nonsense. In the shower? Why would anyone hide when I had been lying asleep, a helpless, perfect victim, for God knew how long? The chair remained lodged under the doorknob. The sound came again. It was regular and mechanical. I spotted the source, the ceiling fan. Every few rotations it caught.

I kicked off my flip-flops, stood on the bed, and pulled the chain to change the speed of the fan. This only caused the cha-chunk to speed up and slow down. If I turned off the fan, my sweat would pickle me like ceviche.

I resettled on the bed and fretted away the night. Would Lalo's friend kill me before I escaped from Zihuatanejo? I drifted into sleep again and dreamed of Hugo Morales's foot on my shoulder, pushing me down, the sun glinting through the water, fish casually gliding by, as I struggled to rise up to the air.

Hugo Morales's weight pressed me toward my death. My hands flailed through heavy water. The fight for my life dragged into slow motion, like a sticky videotape about to snap. Strands of my hair wafted in the water as though I were a mermaid, but one that could drown. The anklebone protruding from Hugo's leg winked in the sunlit water. I opened my mouth to bite it and the water rushed in.

I awoke gasping for breath, my rib cage on fire, the flowered top cover bunched at my sides.

Footsteps. Outside my door on the landing.

I rose carefully from the bed. With my improvised weapon in hand, I glided to the door and watched the knob wiggle.

Then the footsteps retreated. Surely Hugo would not give up this easily? Did he know I was awake? Was this a trap to lure me outside?

I removed the chair-brace from the door. Curiosity killed the cat, but I could not help myself.

I unlocked the door and peeked outside.

The figure wheeled. Startled.

"*Buenas noches,*" the professor said. "I heard a noise." He finished in Spanish that he was checking to see if everything was okay.

I heaved a sigh of relief, but felt guilty to be the cause of his restless night. I hid the lamp behind my back.

"*Gracias. Todo esta bien,*" I lied.

There would be no sleep. I braced the door again and stretched out on the bed.

I thought about the next day. Where would I go? Should I give up the pursuit of my father? If I went home, would David Shapiro welcome me? Would our "time apart" become permanent? Would his friend J.J. Sloan still want me as his employee? J.J. had given me a job because he was David's childhood friend. His agency didn't have enough work to merit two people, but I was only part time, and J.J. liked having someone to whom he could delegate grunt work.

My thoughts turned to the money my mother had left me and how I didn't have to worry about either of my two jobs for a while. Even though my mom had never been the tender, comforting type, or maybe precisely because she had not been that type, her presence had reassured me. Now I felt heartbroken. Grief seized me like a giant bird squeezing me with its talons. I was bereft. If Hugo had killed me, who would even miss me? Lola, maybe, but only because no one would be around to give her teaspoons of ice cream. Tears leaked onto my cheeks. I let them run until they tickled my ears. Then I wiped them away and decided whether my dad was dead or alive, I was going to deliver the letter. What else did I have to do with my life that was meaningful?

I awoke to sun streaming through the opened drapes. I took a long shower, during which the light spray of water went from tepid to cool. I emerged a new woman. My loose damp frizzing hair sprinkled my fresh tee and shorts as I padded about the room, packing my bag.

Removing the chair from under the doorknob, I flip-flopped my way to the office to use the phone. The professor recommended a travel agent and passed the tan rotary phone over the desk. I dialed and the girl who answered sounded young, but her English proved to be excellent.

"You are very lucky," she told me. There was a flight out that day, with seats available, and with one stop in Los Angeles, I could be in Tucson in a mere eight hours.

In less than twenty minutes, I said goodbye to the professor and Rosa and carried my bag across the street to Elvira's for some breakfast since there would be nothing at the tiny airport.

As I repeated my meal of granola and yogurt and fruit, the tang of pineapple cued a memory of a person fleeing up the steps to the kitchen.

I waved over my waiter, a serious fellow named Moses with deep-set, tragic eyes.

"Does a young guy named Hugo Morales work here?" I asked in Spanish.

"Hugo Morales." He kept his hands locked behind his white uniform, never directly met my gaze, and wrinkled his forehead in thought. "A young man named Hugo sells us fish."

"When does he come?"

"Very early," Moses replied.

I looked around uneasily.

"He's not here now," Moses said.

I shot a glance toward Patti's restaurant next door and then scanned the beach. Hugo could be a million places, watching me even now. The taxi stand was a long block away, on the street behind the restaurants and beach action.

I asked Moses if he could call me a cab. As he started to explain the location of the taxi stand only one block away, I impatiently interrupted him. "*Yo sé.*"

He sent a nearby barefoot boy sprinting over the cobblestones. In five minutes a taxi honked its horn at the end of the road behind Elvira's, and in a half hour I was at the Zihuatanejo airport.

The airport consisted of one small terminal and Mark Escalante spotted me as soon as I entered into the blissful air-conditioning. Looking fresh and snappy in his creased khakis and blue Ban-Lon shirt, he sauntered over as I stood in line. "I have a gumshoe on my trail."

I forced a smile. "All the way to Tucson."

"Police run you out of town, too?" He scooted his suitcase, wardrobe bag draped over it, as the line inched forward.

"More like the criminal element. Where are your buddies?"

He nodded at two policemen by the entrance. "What takes you to Tucson?" he asked, suddenly all business.

"The same guy who will no doubt take you back to Zihuatanejo."

He smirked. "Your *friend*, Mr. Get-Out-Of-Jail-Free."

"He's no friend of mine." I stepped up to the counter, greeted the flight attendant in Spanish, and received my middle seat assignment. She glanced at Mark, and even though she was young enough to be his daughter, her eyes sparked.

"I'm already checked in," he said in Spanish that was much smoother than mine. Then he did something that reminded me of why I was not with David Shapiro, why I was down in Mexico alone. He smiled warmly at the flight attendant and asked if it might not be possible for me to have the middle seat by him.

"That's okay," I protested. "My seat is fine."

But I may as well not have spoken. The red acrylic nails clicked over the keyboard.

"Don't worry," he said to me in English. "I'm not trying to pick up on you. This is to protect me from sitting by some fatty or yakaholic."

"Oh, that makes me feel better." I leaned over the counter. "This really isn't necessary," I told the flight attendant.

"It's no problem," she said. "The person in that seat is traveling alone."

"But I don't want to move."

She pulled upright as though to get a better gander at me. "Your seat is back by the toilets."

"Perhaps I could move back by her," Mark offered.

She smiled at him. So gallant. Then she flicked annoyed eyes at me and the growing line.

"That's okay," I sighed, oppressed with the accumulated tiredness from two nights of poor sleep. "I'll move up."

Maybe I would fall asleep and snore on his shoulder.

Mark Escalante followed me to a row of hard plastic chairs. "So Mr. Geraldo Sabala is no longer your friend."

"Nope." I slumped in a seat, rested my feet on my pack and closed my eyes.

He sat beside me, dug in his pack, flipped pages, and settled into a new paperback, a Harlen Coben thriller. As soon as our flight was announced, I lugged my suitcase to the women's room to change into my warmer airplane clothes.

It wasn't until hours later, when we were fighting our way through the hordes and confusion of customs at LAX that he said, "If Geraldo Sabala is not your friend, I take it you would have no problem if I go back for him."

Ahead of us two golden-haired backpackers conversed enthusiastically in a language I didn't recognize. Dutch? Swedish? Behind us was an Indian family, the mother in a sari, their cart piled high with bags. The terminal echoed a cacophony of voices, banging and shuffling suitcases, and indecipherable announcements.

"Now?" I asked.

He laughed, showing his dimples and startling the tired, glum, worried travelers around us. *Those damn dimples.* Even the young blonde backpackers turned and gave him an approving once-over.

I looked away. The churning sea of people and cultures and luggage rendered the custom officials ridiculous, like a line of sandbags against a tsunami.

"I have to finish my current business," Mark said, "and see if there's enough money involved to make the trip worthwhile."

This handsome man had sat in the shade at La Pizza, flirting easily with Geraldo's wife, seeing Geraldo's young daughter in her yellow apron.

He seemed to follow my thoughts. "I'm a bounty hunter, Carol. It's what I do."

"Geraldo Sabala is my brother."

All the other lines moved forward while ours stayed rooted.

"I figured you were related because of the shared last name," Mark Escalante huffed, "but brother, that makes this awkward."

"Half-brother," I amended, not understanding myself. Was I pissed enough at Geraldo to want this man to haul him to the United States to stand trial? He had committed a serious crime and spawned the likes of Lalo de la Cruz and Hugo Morales, one a murderer and the other a wannabe murderer with me as his victim. When I thought of Hugo Morales, my blood boiled. I drew a deep breath. I wanted revenge, but Geraldo was not Hugo.

If I stayed focused on the present, on the here and now, Geraldo hadn't done anything to me. He had even been helpful. Hadn't he sprung me from the hell of a Mexican jail? I craned my neck to see why our line was stalled. I had a knack for picking wrong lines. I invariably chose the one with a customer who needed a price check, or here, perhaps one with a traveler who hesitated on the routine questions. I couldn't see.

"So how much do you care if I pursue your half-brother?" Mark pressed.

"Would it make any difference?"

He shrugged and joined me in peering to the front of our line. Since he had a height advantage, he reported, "Kenyans. The customs official is obviously some stupid new bureaucrat who's never seen a marathon. Probably wonders why blacks from Africa have such expensive running shoes."

The Indian family rolled their cart forward a foot even though our line had not moved. We were in the middle of a snake of people that stretched back to the end of the ropes with a mass of lined up people on both sides. In an emergency, there was no way to move. I felt claustrophobic. My heartbeat quickened, and I burned with anxiety. My face dampened.

Mark bent down to his pack and came up with a sock. "I knew this stray had a purpose."

I dried my face with the sock. "You're a life saver."

He laughed. "Life saver. That's refreshing. I usually get called cowboy or renegade or shithead. And that's by bail bondsmen."

"I'm not surprised. Would you really go back to Mexico?"

"Why not? Because they deported me? Does that stop Mexicans from coming here?"

Our line finally nudged forward, but I still had plenty of time to think about the question I had sidestepped. How much did I care if Mark pursued my half-brother? As a private detective, wasn't I supposed to stand for truth, justice and the American way? And if I didn't stand for that, what did I stand for? Hadn't Geraldo participated in a homicide? What if he were the shooter? He claimed he wasn't, but prisons were stocked with "innocent" criminals. I considered the security guard's family. Their version of the story might sound a lot different.

But what about Geraldo's family, his friendly wife Ana with her gold teeth, and his spunky daughter? The girl who owned my father's heart. I realized that I didn't know her name. My only niece and I had not bothered to inquire. How much did this newly discovered family really mean to me?

On the other hand, if miraculously my father was not dead, and if miraculously I managed to find him, what would I say: "Hi, Dad. Glad to meet you. Guess what I did to your son?"

We finally arrived at the bored, overweight customs official who assumed Mark and I were together. He asked us rote questions about the purpose of our trip to which we both answered, "Vacation," and about the weather in Zihuatanejo, to which we responded, almost in unison, like an old married couple, "Hot." We passed through and trekked to our connecting flight.

As my mom would say, I had a habit of cutting off my nose to spite my face. I had to fight against this tendency in order to see Mark as a resource. He knew Tucson. And in his line of work, he would know the right people. If anyone could help me find my father, it was Mark. This time I chose to sit by him. He wisely did not press me to answer his question about Geraldo.

Once we were settled on the plane, I began my interrogation. "I suppose you know the Tucson medical examiner?"

He nodded. "Of course." He waited.

I waited.

He reached down for his paperback.

"Are you going to tell me his name?"

"You didn't ask."

"Well?"

"And why should I do that?"

"To help a fellow investigator?" With only a little effort, I could locate the ME's name. I was probing Mark's willingness to assist me, and he knew it.

"And what are you investigating? You know, Carol, you told me that you were going to Tucson because of this Geraldo Sabala. How do I know you aren't pursuing his bounty yourself?"

I laughed. For a calculating man, he'd hit so far off the mark. Yet, during our flirtation, during our hellish night in jail, even when I had related my near-death experience, I had never told him the true nature of my search. I had let him infer and speculate, but I had never divulged or shared. He still thought I'd found my man.

In the jet seat, I angled toward the chiseled jaw and deep chest. As I poured out my heart to Mark Escalante, a warm, strong, comforting arm snaked its way around my shoulder.

CHAPTER 31

The Tucson airport was about the same size as the Zihuatanejo airport, small enough that I simply walked through the terminal and down a short hallway to the car rentals.

Mark escorted me even though I assured him it was not necessary. During the plane ride, we had exchanged information. I had his address, home phone, cell phone number, and both home and business e-mail addresses. He had offered me a room in his house. Either this guy was smitten or he wanted to keep an eye on me. Both possibilities made me quiver.

He hovered as I rented my Avis compact and signed that I would not, under any circumstances, take the car into Mexico.

"Is this a problem?" I asked the woman at the counter.

"We're near the border, ma'am," the clerk said tightly. She was older than I and must have had some inkling I didn't want to be ma'amed. "Tourists decide to go to Nogales, and next thing we know, the car is missing." She handed me the key, envelope of paper work, and a map of Tucson.

Mark walked me out to my silver Chevy Prizm in slot E5. The Tucson winter evening was temperate, but felt cold compared to Zihuatanejo.

I tossed my bag into the passenger seat. Mark dropped his to the concrete, stepped in closer and pressed me against the car. His lips went for my throat, a seriously vulnerable spot. He swept my hair back and kissed and murmured his way to my ear, as though he had a treasure map to my erogenous zones.

He slammed shut the car door with his free hand. He whispered in my ear. He could have been reciting nursery rhymes or suggesting unspeakable acts, the warm breath puffing into my ear weakened my knees. The hardness pressed against my thigh excited me, and I reached around to grab his buns, pulling him closer. He nibbled my lips, confidently, gently exploring. He was an expert kisser and I loved kissing.

In the twilight, the parking garage was dim, but a passing family caused him to back away momentarily; I reached down, latched on to a pocket, and tugged him back toward me. A strong arm circled my back, the other swept down to my breast. My nipples stood at attention and he tweaked one, hard like someone in command. "Follow me to my place."

Every inch of my body said yes. In answer, I put my lips to his.

"Get in the car," he said, backing away. "I'll drive."

I hesitated. I reluctantly handed him the key and went around to the passenger seat and pitched my bag into the back. He had his luggage loaded and was backing out before I was buckled in. I ran my hand up his thigh.

I hadn't felt this way since the beginning of my relationship with David. Blood pulsed everywhere in my body; my heart hammered, my fingers tingled, and my face flushed. I wanted to hold on to the thrill of anticipation, a rare sensation in middle age.

But even as Mark sped toward the long-term parking, the energy lessened. As though he could sense it, Mark pushed against my hand, glanced at me, and caressed my face. He shouldn't have demanded the key.

Or maybe the thought of David cooled my heat. For all his annoying pushiness, he accepted me. And he lived in Santa Cruz. What would I do with a lover in Tucson? My body throbbed with desire and told my mind to shut up.

It took only a few minutes to reach his car. Except for my Ghia, I generally regarded vehicles as nothing more than a way to get from here to there. However, J.J. had taught me to take note of makes and models and taillights, a necessity, he argued, in a job where you followed people. But J.J.'s obsession ran deeper; he depleted his wallet every month on a dented silver diesel-spewing wreck so he could say he drove a BMW. Before me stood J.J.'s wet dream, a perfectly maintained black Dodge Charger, just like that of the villain in *Bullitt*. In spite of a thin layer of rain-pocked dust, the curves looked glossy, the rims complicated, expensive and shiny.

Mark clambered out with his luggage, letting in a blast of cold air. "It's not far," he assured me. He started his babe mobile. It rumbled to life. Sexy. Why was I worrying about him being in Tucson? If I wanted a one-night stand, the distance was perfect. But desert air snapped me to attention and pulled Mark into focus—handsome, but cold. Smart, but humorless.

As I walked around my car to the driver's seat, he returned and pushed me against the metal, but the force was a little too rough, and when he kissed my neck, it was like a Bic that didn't flick. He tried the breast. Then he pulled away. "What is this, Carol?"

"I have a boyfriend."

"Boyfriend," he sneered. "I've been with you for days and you haven't mentioned any boyfriend. He couldn't be that important."

I bit my lip and hated him for questioning my lie.

He pressed in for another kiss, but I twisted my head and pushed him away.

He backed up and took a hard look at me. "You're a cock tease." He turned brusquely and strode toward the purring Charger.

I hurried after him.

He spun around. "Change your mind?"

All my pent-up sexual tension and hot lava anger flowed into my arm. I slapped Mark Escalante hard enough to turn his steel jaw.

Before I could feel any afterglow, Mark twisted my body and pinned both of my arms behind my back.

He kissed my neck and whispered in my ear. This time I heard every word. "You try something like that again, you're a dead woman."

I could kick back hard against his shin and probably escape, but I believed his words. I waited for him to release me. He shoved me toward my humiliating little compact, then climbed into his sexy machine and sped away.

CHAPTER 32

Shivering and indignant I sat in my car, staring into the desert night. *Cock tease.* That was so unfair. When had I come on to Mark?

Well there was my *pareo*, the way I hitched the soft fabric around my neck to show off my shoulders and reveal my legs. I had set out to get his attention. Maybe there was some truth in his words, but did I deserve to be called a *cock tease?* I had to get a grip on the bumper car ride of my hormones before I suffered emotional whiplash.

The Tucson winter weather allowed me to sit comfortably in the car for some time. Finally I opened the map from the Avis counter. It showed a logically gridded city, at least a lot more logically gridded than Santa Cruz.

Back on the plane, before he had become the antichrist, Mark had advised me to start my search for my father with the Mexican Consulate. It was downtown, but he had not known the exact address. After I had composed myself, I started the car. I got on a straight north thoroughfare called Kino Boulevard that headed directly toward a mountain range cut out against the crepuscular sky. Its beauty compensated for the flat, unglamorous sprawl of the town. I pulled into a gas station and asked for directions to the Mexican Consulate. The thin, pasty teenager behind the mini-mart counter gave me a blank stare.

"Do you have a phone booth?"

His watery blue eyes looked like they were on break. He scratched at the underarm of his Kid Rock tee shirt unaware how unappetizing that might be to someone out to buy a king-sized Coke and chilidog.

"One of those places where Clark Kent changed into his Superman outfit?" I prodded. Where no one ever stole Clark's suit or wondered if he could be an exhibitionist.

The clerk squinted, as if better to see the prehistoric creature before him, but he pointed outside. I imagined it would not be long before we had a generation who did not understand "phone booth" even with the Superman clue.

And in truth, it wasn't much of a booth, just a counter with Plexiglas sides. Thankfully a phone book was still attached to its chain. I found the Mexican Consulate and the address was listed: 553 S. Stone Ave. Back in my car, I turned on the overhead light and located the street on my map. The Consulate would be closed, but I decided to find it and then pick a hotel nearby, so I could get started with my hunt bright and early the next day.

The streets and turns formed a mantra in my head, trying to drown out the other one: *Cock tease, cock tease, cock tease.* The humiliation lit a spot of fire at the base of my neck. The flames spread slowly upward and downward.

I opened my car window and heard a rumbling engine. I sat bolt upright and inspected the rearview, but a Ford Explorer with tinted windows rose behind me like a wall, so I couldn't see the source of the growling engine. I checked the side mirrors. The Explorer honked at me to move it through a yellow light. I zipped across the intersection, switched lanes, and checked all the mirrors again. The streetlights did not help much. I could not spot even a glimpse of black car, but a powerful, muscle-car engine rumbled through the crisp desert air. No doubt Mark was a pro at tailing; it was part of his job. But why would he bother? He was too cold and too alluring to the opposite sex for one rejection to upset him.

I considered my options. If he was behind me, I could hardly elude him via speed. Evading him by ducking down side streets seemed equally ridiculous. He knew the city; I did not.

I would stick with basics. I closed the car window and locked the doors. I needed to stay in public, well-lighted places.

When I turned on to Stone Avenue, a black Charger did not follow me. Instead a Mustang full of teenagers shot straight on. Even as I breathed a sigh of relief, I worried I was becoming paranoid, an old lady who imagined a bad guy behind every cactus. The traffic was thin on Stone. I pulled to an empty curb in front of the consulate.

A single-story peach stucco building stood behind a wrought iron fence, peaceful in the streetlights. Dramatic cacti adorned a trim lawn. It was much smaller and less official than I had imagined, as though it might have once been someone's home.

I headed toward the downtown area of Tuscon, a nearby cluster of a few high-rises lit up against the dark night. I looked for a hotel rather than a motel. After my sleepless night in Zihua, I wanted a room inside a building. Even though the car following me had not been Mark, I felt jittery. I had come to be in Tucson because of Geraldo's Cucarachas. Did any of them still exist? Could Lalo and Hugo have ties to them? Some of my nervousness, I knew, stemmed from being alone in an unfamiliar place.

The first hotel I spotted was a tall blockish building with several palm trees out front. Normally I would have considered it outside my budget, but my mom's money had changed things for me, and I wasn't in the mood to search for something cheaper looking. Hyper-vigilant, I pulled into the parking garage and chose a space with emptiness around it. After adjusting my bag over my shoulder, I unlocked the door and clutched the car key in my hand as a weapon. I kept my eye on the lot entrance until the elevator door shut, and I didn't fully exhale until I was at the reception desk, asking for a room on the highest floor to get away from the street noise.

After Villas Rosa, the room lacked charm even though it had a nice view over the twinkling lights of downtown to dark silhouettes of distant mountains. But who needed charm? All I wanted was a good night's sleep.

The next morning, I faced the quandary of what to wear. I'd packed for the tropics, not the high desert. When I opened the hotel window to test the temperature, the sun was out but the air was cool, hardly shorts weather. Pale blue sky snapped the distant mountains into a sharp focus of dark blue. Snow traced their cooler crevices. With mountain views in almost every direction, I could see why people would like this city.

I sniffed my one set of warm clothes that I had worn on the plane to and from Mexico. If I wore the Levi's and my only long-sleeved shirt, I would have to stand at least a yard away from anyone I met, but since I didn't plan any more encounters like the one with Mark, I put them on.

In the light of day, my nervousness about Mark Escalante and being in a new city had diminished. I ate scrambled eggs in the hotel restaurant and decided to walk to the Mexican Consulate. If Mark wanted to find me, he certainly knew where I would go. He had been the one to suggest the idea. But he could not possibly care that much about me.

The hotel sat beside a park, but the rest of the walk was less lovely. I had expected Tucson to possess more Southwest charm—more adobe, xeriscaping and *ristras* of *chiles*, but other than the mountains that ringed it, with three prominent points off to the west, the city had the flat urban sprawl that could be Anywhere, USA. I walked at my usual long-legged gallop and covered the distance to the Mexican Consulate in about six minutes.

Even in the bright morning light, the building exuded a peaceful, deserted aura. No one drove up or went in or out. I entered with the only useful information I possessed: the photo of Geraldo Sabala with his granddaughter.

Inside, the consulate embraced the cool, musty aroma of bureaucracy, of dust motes undisturbed by much motion other than the sound waves of ringing phones. Between calls, a young receptionist attentively listened to the abbreviated account of what I wanted and directed me to the Protection Department at the back of the building.

The man in the office greeted me formally in accented, very correct English. Slim, immaculately groomed, and fragrant, he wore an elegantly tailored gray suit with a starched white shirt and silky gray, blue and red striped tie. His dress shoes could serve as mirrors. Judging on appearance, he was a step-up from the typical American bureaucrat. Ignoring his ringing phone, he invited me to sit, returned to his desk, and listened as I explained my quest.

"You say this missing person was from Naco, Mexico?" he asked.

"Yes."

"If he crossed there, you should direct your inquiry to the Mexican Consulate in Douglas." He straightened a stack of papers that were already straight.

Maybe he wasn't so different from an American bureaucrat, after all. He would be more than happy to pass this work along to someone else. "His son said I should start here. He thinks his father crossed into this county."

"Pima County," he offered. "Didn't you say the missing person was your father?"

"Yes." This was not the time to waffle with I think so. Instead, I presented the theory of my father's past as fact.

The tale held the young man's attention. He ignored his office phone and only made me wait when his cell phone rang. He had a quick affectionate conversation in Spanish. He promised to call back in five minutes, so I knew exactly how much more time he planned to spend with me.

The need to call back in five minutes spurred him into action. He took out a legal pad and asked me questions about my dad: Name? Birth date? Height? Weight?

I didn't know the last two, but offered reasonable guesses from the photos I'd seen.

Eyes?

I assumed brown.

Dental Work?

Clueless.

Tattoos?

"I don't think he had any tattoos, but the side of his cheek was scarred. He had a mustache." I handed him the photo. Then I remembered a conversation with Geraldo. "Broken collarbone."

"May I keep this?"

I reluctantly nodded and he paper clipped the photo to his notes. "What happens next?" I asked.

"Someday we hope to have this all on computer, but for now I have to take your information and start making contacts, the hospitals, jails, detention facilities, Border Patrol. . . ."

I interrupted him. "So you can't investigate based on the assumption he might be dead?"

"No. We have to proceed like he's a missing person." He patted down his tie.

His statement failed to stir any hope in me. I had started to accept Geraldo's belief my father was dead. The young man's words caused a sinking feeling. The Mexican Consulate was beginning at square one and this could be a long, tedious affair.

"Would it be possible for you just to make a copy of that photo?" I asked.

He scrunched his smooth face, a quick moue, and checked his watch. "It won't be as accurate."

"This is the last request, and I'm gone," I reassured him.

He liked the sound of that and smoothing his tie, rose from his desk to comply.

CHAPTER 33

I needed to talk to someone who worked with dead people.

I retraced my steps to the hotel, went to my room and sniffed my armpits. I decided to exchange reek for goose bumps and pulled on an unworn aqua tank top. I would be driving to the Medical Examiner's Office anyway, so what did it matter that it was sixty degrees out?

Before I left, I made up my mind to call La Pizza to warn Geraldo about Mark Escalante. At this point the rat wouldn't feel any need for approval to hunt down my brother. I searched all the pockets of my clothing and dug to the bottom of every crevice in my suitcase, but the business card from La Pizza was gone.

I went to the lobby, borrowed a phone book, and looked up International Calling, which seemed useful only if one already knew a number. Leaning on the counter, I checked Operator Assistance. Apparently, I needed to dial 00. While I had the phone book, I tracked down the address of the Medical Examiner's office. Using the hotel's pen, I scribbled the info on the back of the hotel's business card.

Back in my room, I sat on the rumpled bed, thinking of Mark's whispered words, "You ever try something like that again, you're a dead woman."

I massaged my tender rib. Would he consider my phone call equivalent to slapping him? Mark's words dispelled any ambivalence I felt regarding Geraldo's past life of crime. Plus, any injury Geraldo had caused me via Hugo was oblique and from a long time ago, while Mark Escalante's injury was up close and personal. The enemy of my enemy was my friend.

This feeling didn't extend all the way to Hugo Morales, though. If there was a bounty on that piece of shit, Mark was welcome to it, but Geraldo had some redeeming features. He had sprung me from jail. He had a lovely wife and child. And he was my half-brother.

I dialed 00, and listened through a phone tree of impossible options since I didn't have a calling card, wasn't making a collect call, and couldn't reverse the charges to my home phone since no one would answer. At the end of the tree, I waited for a live person.

She sounded less personable than the recording. I told her what I wanted.

"Just a moment."

After several seconds, a phone rang. Then the phone squawked and an annoying, nasal voice told me that if I needed help, I should hang up and dial the operator.

I called 411, and a live male told me he couldn't help me, to try the 00. I explained what had happened. He suggested I call 0.

After the kind of experience that made shooting rampages understandable, I emerged victorious with the number for La Pizza. At times stubbornness was a very fine quality to possess.

I dialed. The phone rang and rang. Under a bunch of crackling, Ana answered.

I identified myself in loud, clear Spanish.

"Yes?" Ana asked. She didn't offer any *saludos*. Even over the static, I sensed wariness. Certainly she wasn't her friendly, chatty self. Pots banged in the background.

"Could I speak to Geraldo?" I shouted in Spanish.

"He isn't here."

"Is he at home?"

"He's gone." She sounded angry.

"Gone where?"

There was no response except the crackle of bad connection. "Hello, Ana?"

"Yes."

"Where has Geraldo gone?"

Silence and crackling. She either didn't know where he'd gone or didn't want to tell me, in which case she was too polite to hang up or too honest to lie.

"This is because of you," Ana said.

"Because of me?" I wasn't sure I had understood the Spanish correctly. Talking on the phone challenged my second language ability.

"That guy you brought to La Pizza."

Mark? I started to protest that I hadn't brought anyone to the restaurant. Was Geraldo gone because of Mark? Even before I'd left Zihua, Geraldo had picked up on the eau de cop. If he'd disappeared because of it, then Ana was right. Mark Escalante had followed me to Geraldo. If it weren't for me, Mark may not have ever noticed him.

"Did you tell Geraldo he talked to you at the restaurant?"

"Yes," she sniffled. "And that man called. He didn't say it was him, but I know it was him."

I froze, swearing internally. Everything I did, Mark Escalante was one step ahead. The snake.

If Geraldo sensed Mark had him in his crosshairs, it was no wonder he had fled. Look what had happened to his buddy Lalo de la Cruz. Did Mark know that Ana had told Geraldo about their encounter in the restaurant. Or, would Mark think that I had tipped him off? And why not? Here I was about to do it.

I bent down and probed the cut on my ankle. The pain kept me alert. Mark must have known a call was risky, but on the other hand, if Geraldo had answered, he could have simply hung up, safe in the knowledge that his prey was still in Zihuatanejo and that another trip to Mexico wouldn't be for nothing.

I didn't have the Spanish or the inclination to argue with Ana that it wasn't my fault, that Mark was trained to identify people; his livelihood depended on recognizing faces attached to rewards. Besides, part of me knew the current situation was my fault. I had piqued Mark's interest in my quarry and then had led him right to the man. I concentrated on trying to explain to Ana that I had called to warn Geraldo. I didn't have the proper vocabulary for that, either, and had to resort to *policía* for bounty hunter.

Ana stayed quiet.

"Did Geraldo go to Naco?" I guessed.

A possible sob punctuated the static and then a click.

I remained on the unmade bed and considered my options. If I called back, I doubted Ana would answer. And I had delivered my message. Too late. But at least for now Geraldo had escaped Mark's grasp.

I opened my map of Tucson and memorized my route to the Medical Examiner's office. As I drove, my eyes flicked to the mirrors. No black Charger. Twenty minutes later I pulled up to the brown single-story cement block building.

The receptionist informed me that the Medical Examiner was occupied, but I could talk to an investigator.

If the Medical Examiner was with a body, I might have to wait for hours. "That would be excellent," I told her.

A tall, rangy guy dressed in cowboy boots, Levi's and a USA tee shirt appeared from the hallway. He sported a gray ponytail and a mustache, bushy like my father's, but gray. "Hiya, I'm Sam."

His blue eyes twinkled, his greeting was energetic and his handshake firm, but I still expected him to call me "sweetheart" or "dear" when he indicated a seat in his office. "What can I do you for?"

"About six million and twenty-four cents."

Since he grinned at my retort, I forgave him the line, and rendered a quick version of what I wanted.

"So you believe your father died in our desert and ended up as a John Doe?" He leaned back in his desk chair, which protested, and clasped both hands on top his head. "And when did this supposedly happen?"

"Probably in the last six months."

He regarded me skeptically, lowered his hands and shook his head. "Didn't happen."

"How can you say that just like that?" I snapped my fingers.

He leaned toward me. His stare lost its twinkle. I braced myself for a "dear."

"Because I know we don't have an older, male, Caucasian John Doe for the last half of 1998 in our files," he said.

I handed him the photo. "This is my father."

He barely glanced at it, and then did a double take. "Your father is Hispanic?"

"Mexican," I confirmed, realizing this needed to be part of my preamble: I am looking for my Mexican father. Otherwise, people made the same assumption the investigator had—that I was white through and through.

"Well, that changes things."

He went to a file cabinet. "Ever since they started Operation Gatekeeper in California and Hold the Line in El Paso, our Mexican John Does have been on the rise. At the rate we're going, I hate to think what it will be like in a few years." He tossed a manila folder in front of me, a guy untroubled by rules. "There are ten or so in there, most of them young, but there are a couple of older guys. Would you like some coffee?"

I could only imagine what the office coffee might be like, but it couldn't be worse than the black paste we served at J.J. Sloan's Investigative Services. I said yes to be polite. "Black." Maybe it would warm me up; goose bumps pocked my bare arms.

I watched him out the door.

I eagerly turned my attention to the folder. I had thought I might be through by the time Sam returned with the coffee, but I was still on the first male, estimated to be in his young twenties based on a "visual assessment of the morphological changes of the pubic symphyseal face." I couldn't pull myself away from the report, the list of body parts found. Although couched in cool, scientific terms, the body had been ripped apart and eaten, the bones scoured clean by bugs and scorching sun. There was "no dental work," only several teeth showing signs of decay. No clothing, no jewelry, no I.D. About as anonymous as a John Doe could get.

Sam sat a Styrofoam cup in front of me and glanced over my shoulder. "Welp, I won't warn you about the coffee. You obviously have a strong stomach."

He reseated himself, tipped back in his chair, the spring squeaking a little, and read pink message slips. He tore one into tiny pieces. "Ex-wife," he explained as he sprinkled pink snow into the garbage can by the file cabinet.

I sipped the coffee. It was hot and burnt. I skimmed the next report. "What's a pubic symphyseal face?"

"It's the anterior pelvic bone joint. You'll see that a lot when we have skeletal remains for an adult, and out in the desert it doesn't take long before all we have is bones."

"Is that joint a pretty accurate way to tell age?"

Sam folded his arms over his chest and barked a nice, bitter guffaw. "Completely subjective." He rocked and the padded gray desk chair squeaked. "We visually compare the bone in hand to a series of casts."

"Where do the remains go?"

"If someone steps up to claim them, we have a funeral parlor that specializes in repatriation."

"And if no one does?" My warmed fingertips left depressions in the thin paper of the reports.

"They become John Does in the county cemetery."

I skipped to the next report. Sam tore up another pink message. Then he started on his answering machine messages. The first person had not even finished identifying herself before he pushed the delete button.

"Reporter," he explained.

His efficient office management style left me somewhere between admiring and appalled.

The page under my fingertips discussed another Hispanic male in his late twenties, but this time the body was intact, the death estimated to have occurred within the previous hour of the report, approximately one o'clock in the morning. The cause of death translated to one bullet in the back and blood loss. One bullet often didn't kill a person, but the man had lain for an hour pumping blood into the sand.

I couldn't stop reading. I summarized aloud. A rancher had found him on a ranch road along with another older Hispanic male, possibly in his sixties, with a head wound.

"Do you remember this case?"

"Of course," Sam said before I pushed the manila folder across the desk. He skimmed it. "Some sort of crazy shootout. A person might think a drug deal gone bad, except the two victims were unarmed."

"Is there another report in here for the older guy?"

Sam shook his head. "Nope."

"Why not?"

"He wasn't dead."

My heartbeat quickened. "He was shot in the head?"

"Yeah, but he only had a depression fracture."

I picked at the edge of the paper. "His head was dented and cracked?"

"Pretty much," Sam said. "That can happen if the bullet grazed him and he fell on a rock, or he was turning his head, or he was wearing something like a leather hat. Bullets do all kinds of weird shit when they hit a body." He trailed off, seeming to realize what we might be discussing.

"What happened to him?"

"TMC, probably. Tucson Medical Center." Sam stopped all movement. Then he unspiked one of the phone messages he had deigned to keep, glanced at it, and sketched some rough directions on the back. "It's not far."

I pressed my hand to my heart as though I meant to say The Pledge to his patriotic tee shirt.

He handed me the pink slip. I forced myself to remain seated and to glance through the rest of the file even as my heart revved into full gear.

There was another possibility: John Doe number fourteen, with an estimated age of late fifties to early sixties, the cause of death dehydration. He had been found in a shallow grave marked with a cross made of sticks.

Someone had cared about him and had watched him die an agonizing death. And all for what? To plead for work in a Home Depot parking lot?

I was getting a feel for some of the main thoroughfares in this part of Tucson. My hotel was on Broadway. I took it to Swan to reach the huge Medical Center. I nervously watched and listened for Mark Escalante's Charger. If he thought I'd tipped off Geraldo Sabala, if he thought I knew where Geraldo had gone, Mark Escalante would track me to the gates of hell. He was the type who always got his man.

As I squinted at the medical complex signage, I realized I didn't have anything resembling a plan. I had to suck in deep breaths to prevent hyperventilation. I found a parking space, available because both of the adjacent SUVs crowded the lines. Feeling smug, I guided the compact into the narrow slot and crawled out the narrowly cracked door.

I rubbed my arms against the brisk air and hustled into the hospital, where I screeched to a halt. Did I ask for information and call attention to myself or did I try to find this John Doe on my own? Was the man still a John Doe? Could he still be here? I pushed away the question of whether he could be my father. That thought caused a cold sweat.

Once upon a time in Dominican Hospital in Santa Cruz I had located a patient by patrolling the corridors, but my home-town hospital was familiar. Furthermore, in that case, I had known exactly who I was looking for. Here I was assuming the John Doe was my father, but even if he was my father, I had seen only a few old photographs on which to base his appearance.

I marched up to the information desk. "Do you have any John Does here?"

My bluntness earned me a wary inspection from both a seated plain-clothes older woman and a standing uniformed nurse.

"We have two," the nurse said. "Both illegal aliens."

Illegal aliens. Illegal was factual and fair enough, but aliens suggested creatures from Mars with bug eyes and attenuated fingers. "If they are John Does, how do you know they are illegal?"

This question sent their shoulders up to their ears and garnered me an eye-roll from the older woman and a hard, suspicious stare from the nurse.

I tried for a softer tone. "This man is older and suffered a gunshot wound to the head."

"Do you know who he is?" the nurse asked hopefully. She was a gray-haired, stocky, no-nonsense woman.

"Maybe."

She checked me over. "Aren't you cold?"

I nodded.

Apparently not finding anything suspicious beyond my inappropriate dress, she motioned for me to follow her. My heart pounded. I felt as though I were floating over the glossy tile into hospital fumes. The antiseptic and bouquets of flowers could never quite mask the smell of blood and diapers, despair and decay.

"These illegal aliens cost this hospital a lot of money," she said crisply.

"The hospital pays for them?" I asked numbly, unable to concentrate on her words, but wanting her to talk so that she would keep moving forward.

"Well, the Border Patrol doesn't have any medical budget," she huffed. "And they don't arrest these people if they're injured. They say it's because they can't risk the time to question them, but we don't get any federal money for housing their detainees."

"This man had a gunshot to the head," I protested.

She sighed. "Well, in this case, I understand. We have the only Level 1 trauma center in Arizona," she added proudly. "But we get guys in here like the other John Doe who has nothing wrong but a broken leg, and he won't even tell us his name."

She stopped abruptly. "So you think you can identify this older John Doe?"

I shrugged.

"Are you a reporter?"

I thought for a second. "Yes."

"What paper?"

"Actually I'm from Santa Cruz, California." The best way to lie was to tell the truth, and I wanted her to continue walking. "My name is Carol Sabala."

"Santa Cruz?"

"Have you heard of it?"

She resumed walking, but less briskly. "Liberal," she stated. An L word. Like liver, lice and loathing.

"We prefer progressive."

She gave me a look like I was being cheeky. "So what paper do you write for?"

"The *Santa Cruz Sentinel.*"

She stopped. "Well, this won't be much of an interview. This guy says less than the John Doe with the broken leg."

"I would still like to see him," I insisted nervously.

She inspected me with intelligent dark eyes. Unconvinced dark eyes. "You do have some lead on this guy?"

"Yes, I do."

"That would be helpful," she said. "He should have been released a long time ago."

"Why hasn't he been?"

"Unlike some places, we don't dump the indigent on the street." With a quickened pace and stiff back, she continued to lead me through a maze of hallways. "What angle are you taking in your story?" she asked, playing along with my Carol Sabala, crack reporter line.

"The burden hospitals shoulder to care for illegal immigrants."

She stopped again and smiled tightly. "We offer quality medical care to anyone who comes through the door," she said coolly, "but these people cost us millions."

I should have let the comment pass and made nice, but I couldn't help myself. "It's not like this guy chose to get shot in the desert. He didn't even choose to come here."

"I know that," she snapped. "But he did make choices."

True, we all made choices, but we weren't all presented with the same choices to make.

"We can't dispense free medical care and continue to operate. Maybe when there are no hospitals left for Americans, people will get the idea." She marched down the hall, waved me inside a room, and then to my dismay, followed me to the first bed.

I stared at the old man. New hairs sprouted from a pale, shaved head except where a red scar ran along the side. His skin was white, his eyes shut, his head flopped to one side near a wet spot on the pillow.

"Did he have a mustache?"

"Yes. A very bushy one," she volunteered. "We shaved it to make his care easier."

I tried to visualize the lifeless face with a mustache and thick salt and pepper hair. "Is he . . . "

"In a coma? He was at the beginning. After that, he had a staph infection." She heaved a sigh. "He's cognizant now, but like I said, he speaks even less than the other guy."

"Is he able to speak?"

"Oh, yes," she said resentfully. "He's slow, but he can speak."

"Can I touch him?"

"Touch him?" she asked skeptically.

"I just need to see the other side of his face."

Something told me that if he were a white man, she would have said no, but in this situation, if I could I.D. this man and help free up the bed for a billable U.S. citizen, she was all for it. I walked around the bed and lifted the head. It was heavy as a bowling ball. I turned it gently. Smooth, shiny scar tissue laced the plane of his cheek.

I almost dropped the head. I bit my lip, but tears still pooled in my eyes. Various emotions rushed in, creating a quagmire of confusion. I needed to back away and to sit alone in a corner for about a half hour, or twenty years, to sort things out.

"So you recognize him?" the nurse asked eagerly.

Along with my damp palms and pounding heart and teary eyes were mixed thoughts of a hundred thousand dollars in medical bills and a life caring for a zombie I didn't know, if he didn't go to jail for human trafficking. I shook my head. Call me Judas.

The nurse patted Geraldo Sabala's cheek. His eyelashes fluttered. I stepped back. What I really wanted to do was bolt from the room. Did she expect him to wake, and in an unguarded moment, to call out my name? He hadn't seen me since I was a baby.

"This is Nurse Grace," she said softly to my father. "You have a visitor."

The eyes opened, warm brown, fuzzy with sleep and uncomprehending. One eye looked a bit droopy. Nurse Grace repeated herself in Spanish and pointed a finger at me.

The head didn't move, but the eyes rolled. They froze, focused, widened, blinked and stared. His lips parted. "Bea." My mother's name. More a moan than a word. My body jumped out of my skin. He probably would not have recognized me in a hundred years, but I stood before him now like an apparition of his first wife. He must have thought he was seeing a ghost.

The nurse encouraged him. "Be what?"

The eyes turned to the nurse. They rolled back toward me, alert now, and snapping with intelligence. The sheet moved infinitesimally, a finger, a hand, inching, yearning.

Nurse Grace watched in wonder. "He recognizes you."

The hand reached the edge of the sheet.

"He wants to hold your hand."

I offered my hand to my father and like a baby he grasped my index finger, the grip surprisingly strong. His eyes grew moist. "*M'ija?*"

The word skewered my heart.

"You're his daughter?" the nurse asked. Her inspection bounced from me to my dad and back, weighing the apparent lack of shared DNA.

My father's eyes hardened, the cunning eyes of a desert animal. "No."

For once in my life I was glad I did not resemble my father. For once in my life I understood and appreciated why he wasn't claiming me.

I shook my head. "I must remind him of someone." I was a Judas to the core.

CHAPTER 34

My father tightly gripped my finger.

"What happens to him next?"

"Shouldn't you get out a recorder or a notepad?" the nurse asked.

That's right, I remembered, I was supposed to be a reporter. When possible, though, I avoided a purse, so all I had was my driver's license, credit card, and some bills stuffed in the pocket of my Levi's. "I have a photographic memory."

She smiled thinly. "Well, what happens next depends on establishing who he is." She tucked the blankets around him. "If he has family, we would like to find them. Someone needs to take him." She scanned my face.

The warm hand squeezed my finger. I remained mute and impenetrable.

"He is aware of his surroundings. He's making good physical progress, walking the hallway without assistance. He should have been moved to a nursing home or a rehab facility a long time ago. Some B.I. patients eventually recover fully."

"B.I.?"

"Brain injury."

The hand squeezed again as though to reassure me.

"What if no one claims him?" I thought of a coat left after a party. Abandoned pets looking forlornly through the bars at the SPCA.

"If we can establish he's a Mexican national, he will probably be deported, if the law doesn't want him. People from the sheriff's department came around at first, but he stayed in a coma long enough for them to lose interest. Now he can feed himself. He goes to the bathroom by himself. We walk him up and down the halls at least twice a day. It's all a slow process, but he can do it. So any day now we will release him to the streets." She gave me a hard look. "He would be better off with home care."

"And if he's a legal?"

"Then he could go to a rehab facility or nursing home and if necessary to residential care for the brain injured." She sighed. "But no one wants him if they won't get paid. Someone has to go through the reams of paperwork to get him on SSI or Medicare."

What was my father's status? Had he ever obtained a green card? How long were they valid? Surely his subsequent marriage in Mexico had invalidated whatever status he had gained via marriage to my mom. I doubted that he had been able to go through the arduous task of becoming a citizen before being driven from the United States.

"Could I talk to the patient alone?"

"Sure," she said. "But he tires easily, so no more than ten minutes." She glanced at her watch and then at the wall clock.

I listened for her departure and watched the red second hand click away a minute. Damn those soft-soled nurse's shoes. I tugged at my finger and Geraldo released his grip. I tiptoed to the door and checked the bright hallway. An aide rolled a food cart to a room down the hall, and two nurses stood in the hallway chatting, but there was no sign of Grace.

I returned to bedside. "Do you know your name?" I whispered.

"Geraldo Sabala," he said slowly and carefully. He raised his hand. I sat on the chair by the bed, the chair for visitors that had no doubt remained empty since his arrival. He pressed a trembling hand to my cheek. "¿M'ija?"

I placed my hand on top of his fingers. "Sí, Carolina Guadalupe Sabala." The name sounded strange to me. I couldn't remember the last time I had pronounced the whole official thing out loud.

My father's eyes pooled with tears. "You look just like your mother."

His hand slid and I guided it back to the bed. Even after months in the hospital, his skin was rough with calluses on the meaty fingertips. His thick fingernails had been bluntly clipped.

I didn't blame him for withholding his name. In the United States he had been treated by a Level I trauma unit, had survived a bullet wound that had cracked his skull, whereas in a Mexican hospital, his wife had died in childbirth. Yet, from the nurse's information, it sounded like he would have been brought here whether a U.S. citizen or a Mexican national. The big issue was what would happen now.

He warily glanced about the room. He motioned for me to bend down. He raised dry lips toward my ear and whispered, "Do you hate me?"

I shook my head. But in a moment of sharp clarity, I realized my mother had. The coded message Donald and I had received was that she didn't love him, possibly had never loved him, and we weren't supposed to love him either.

"I try to come back."

I pulled away. "I know."

He looked around the room again, checked the clock, and said quietly and urgently, "I am coyote."

I nodded. A coldness descended on me. I knew that, but the information had not immediately jibed with the image before me—the old man, the pale, scarred head, my father. Nor did that fact explain why he withheld his name. A district attorney wouldn't need a name to charge him with human trafficking. Of course, that was a difficult case to make if the evidence had run away.

With a start, I remembered that not all the evidence had disappeared. My father had been found with a dead man, shot in the back. My father could be in serious trouble. If he had priors, if he'd even been deported before, the sentencing guidelines for any crime could be stiffer, but without a name, the sheriff's department may have a difficult time digging up his background. Withholding his name was the act of a cunning criminal. For a moment I regarded him as a coyote.

Then he asked, "Bea?"

"She passed away. Recently."

"Donald?"

I willed myself not to cry. "Ten years ago." As though struck by lightning, my heart cracked. All the encrusted pain loosened and spilled out. The memory of my brother's death had been zapping me, sudden and hot, for years, but never with as much force as now. I leaned against the white bedcover and sobbed.

I cried for my fatherless baby self, and my sullen fatherless teenaged self, and the thirty-three year old who lost her brother, and the forty-two year old whose mother died. I cried for my dead brother who never knew his father.

But I was crying for something deeper, too. My journey had led me here. I had located Geraldo Sabala's father, but I couldn't, didn't, feel like I had found mine. We were separated by decades of white empty space. The person before me was a coyote, a stranger with a saggy eye in a hospital bed. He could not miraculously fill the void.

I kept my head down, hot with embarrassment, even as the tears subsided. The situation reminded me of when I was ten and traveled to meet my grandmother in Wisconsin. Even though blood ties made us both eager to meet, and even though, as my mom would say, we both "put our best foot forward," the actual encounter had fallen just short of disastrous. Awkward at best. I was a natural contrarian and my grandmother was a natural disapprover.

Geraldo Sabala lifted his hand to the top of my head and rested it tenderly on my hair. "*M'ija.*"

Nurse Grace cleared her throat.

My father retracted his hand. I jerked upright and wiped my eyes.

Nurse Grace aimed a steely gaze at us. "So he is your father."

I opened my mouth, but she stepped into the room and wagged a finger at me. "No more lies."

I gulped and didn't say anything. My father didn't say anything.

"Look," she said striding to the bed, "I don't mean to be impertinent, but is he married to your mother?"

I put my hands in my lap and waited for my father to take the lead. His lips tightened in silence.

What could either of us say? Yes he had been married to my mother, but he had married a Mexican woman, too. Besides being a coyote, he was a polygamist.

She drilled me with her eyes. "Your mother is an American, right?"

This felt like a safe question to answer. "Yes."

"Then if Mr. John Doe here is married to her, he's probably a legal resident."

I neither denied nor confirmed.

"I'm not trying to get either of you in trouble," she said in exasperation. "I'm only trying to get a little money for the hospital. If we can establish the patient is an indigent legal resident, we can be partially reimbursed for all this." She gestured vaguely at the room—the television, the stainless steel food tray, and the crisp sheets.

I felt guilty, but remained mum. There was no guard on the door, so the sheriff's department obviously did not like my father as the shooter of the young man in the desert. Still, no matter what the nurse said, as a U.S. resident my father could face prison time for human smuggling. As a John Doe Mexican, to save everyone a lot of time and trouble, he might simply be deported.

"Come on," she said brusquely to me. "That's enough time. He's tired."

"I'll come back this afternoon," I whispered in his ear.

He nodded and his lips hinted at a smile.

In the parking lot, my eyes shot around for a black car. It was bad enough that I had led Mark Escalante to Geraldo Sabala, junior. I certainly didn't want Mark Escalante following me to my father and trying to shake him down for information.

"Looking for me?" Mark popped up from the far side of the white Bronco pulled in tightly next to my compact.

"Holy shit!" I pressed the button to unlock the car and squeezed inside. I slammed shut the door and locked it before he could reach me.

He tapped on the window and laughed. Like a maverick, he was dressed in a tight-fitting black tee and snug black jeans. He wore a rattlesnake cowboy hat and cowboy boots, and looked like a country music star enjoying a practical joke.

"Come on, Carol," he said. "Open the window."

"Fuck off."

"Is that any way to treat a near miss?"

He had been a near miss, and I could see why: the chiseled features, the black fabric tracing lines of muscle, the wily intelligence. Just when I had let down my guard, here he was. I didn't trust myself. Nausea roiled in my gut.

He squatted down the best he could in the narrow space so his face was even with mine. "Clearly you mistook me for someone else, and I mistook you for someone else."

I considered his words. Had I expected him to behave like David Shapiro, who would have been ruthlessly on my side? But even David Shapiro didn't take my side when I was in disagreement with him.

Mark tapped the window so I would look at him. "This is business. I just want to ask you a couple of questions about Geraldo Sabala. Then I'll leave you alone." He raised two fingers. "Scouts' honor."

I raised one finger and started my engine.

I wished I could have roared away, but I had to back out

very carefully and then thread through the parking lot, back to the street that took me out to Swan.

Even as I rode the elevator up to my hotel room, I felt shaken, half expecting Mark to ambush me on the landing. He was right. I had allowed myself to fantasize, to change him into a romantic hero, when he had never presented himself as anything other than a bounty hunter, a career in which one had to be cold, determined, and cunning.

Once I was safely locked in my room, I collected the pink envelope. I had traveled over a thousand miles to deliver this letter and yet it didn't seem right to zoom back to the hospital with it. I needed a little time to reflect on my encounter with my father, and I imagined my father needed time to absorb my sudden appearance, too. Plus the watchful Nurse Grace had shooed me from the hospital.

I was too restless and jumpy to stay cooped up, but killing time was difficult in a sterile ten-by-twelve hotel room. If I were outdoors, what difference would it make if Mark followed me? He wouldn't learn anything new, and he wasn't going to assault me out in public.

I ventured outside into the fresh desert air and walked across a pedestrian bridge to a large plaza with a rectangular fountain in its center. The plaza appeared to be Tucson's civic center, urban attractive with patches of grass, large round planters, and patchworks of brick to break up the concrete.

At the end of the plaza rose a building with a beautiful mosaic dome.

I approached the Pima County Courthouse. An arched window topped an elaborately carved archway, but the building's wings, blocky and ordinary, extended from each side. The green and gold geometric patterns of the dome glittered in the sun. The architecture was strikingly discordant and matched my mood.

I sat at the edge of the splashing fountain. Even though I wasn't ready to call Geraldo Sabala *Papi*, I accepted the potency of biology. Some things had been decided for me when his sperm had wiggled its way up to my mother's egg. I was curious what those qualities might be. Were they blocky and ordinary like the sides of the courthouse, or ornate and crowned like the entrance? Even with its contradictions, it was, overall, an appealing building.

I relaxed back on the ledge of the fountain in the mild sunshine, melting under the accumulated tension and exhaustion of the last few days. I massaged my rib, which still hurt when I bothered to pay attention to it. Occasionally I opened a slit of eye to cast about for Mark Escalante. The patter of the fountain calmed me, but after a while it became the sound of irritating nonsense, asking me what I was doing lazing about, until finally, like an alarm, it propelled me into action. I hurried back to my room, retrieved the envelope, descended to the garage, and drove to the hospital.

This time I had the advantage of being able to walk directly to Geraldo Sabala's room, with an eye out for Mark Escalante and Nurse Grace. With any luck, her shift had ended.

I found my father asleep. I watched the mystery of him, his eyes moving behind the lids to some secret dream. Did he see his granddaughter climbing into his lap? Did he relive the blast to his head? Was he remembering his two lost children?

After ten minutes, I turned on the television. I glanced on the other side of the dividing curtain. An old man hooked to an I.V. rested in the bed. He looked dead. I lowered the volume, and taking up residence in the one chair, watched mind-rotting daytime television, a sad parade of humanity willing publicly to air their dirty laundry: petty thefts and infidelity, unbelievable and unwise retributions, hurt feelings and indignation. Were they revealing themselves to the world for their fifteen minutes of fame or were they driven by other motives, perhaps a longing for justice?

Could television court satisfy that longing? I could grasp law and order, crime and punishment, but justice was more abstract. It bubbled in our blood, a deep primal desire, more a matter of the heart than of the courts. Even the drama of television court didn't quench the thirst for justice. Out of the chamber, a wild-eyed defendant stabbed long, curled purple fingernails at the camera to emphasis her much-bleeped protest of the judge's ruling.

My father's eyelashes finally fluttered. The lids lifted. He smiled to see me. A bit lop-sided. He used a button to raise his bed and reached for the glass of water on his tray. I watched him drink. So far I had not seen him do anything with his left hand. He reminded me of a stroke victim—struggling for each action, fighting for each word.

I stood up to show him the pink envelope with his name on the front. I didn't know what to call this man. *Papi* was too intimate, dad too American, Geraldo too separate. "Mom left this for me to give to you." I extracted the envelope stuck inside the pink envelope. "Would you like me to read it to you?"

He touched the duct tape and grinned. Then he sank back to his pillow and nodded.

I ripped open the second envelope and unfolded a sheet of binder paper. The letter was written in Spanish by the hand of a child learning cursive. I was startled to see the date October 10, not long before my mom had died. This moment had come so close to never happening. The letter started with the formal greeting *Estimado* Geraldo Sabala.

The writer introduced herself as Lupita Peralta and said that her teacher was showing them how to write letters that she promised to deliver.

How had the pink envelope, unstamped and unaddressed, ended up in my mother's former Ferndale mailbox. This letter did not promise to solve that mystery. It was a *milagro*. A miracle.

Lupita thanked my father for bringing her to *Los Estados Unidos*. At first she had been afraid of him because of the scars on his face, but people from her village had said he was an honest coyote.

Lupita also wanted to make a confession. She had stolen his pack of gum. When the family was walking across the desert, she discovered the Ferndale address.

She prayed that he was not dead. They heard the gunshots but her father would not let them go back. If this letter reached his hands, she wanted him to know how grateful the family was for his help, how happy they were to have found a man who would protect them, a man like her own father.

It was a long letter for a child.

Her father had found work in the fields and her mother worked in a cannery, but it was going to close and move to Mexico. She and her brother and sister were all in school. She had a very nice teacher, *una rubia*, who could speak Spanish. She, Lupita Peralta, was going to grow up and become a teacher like her.

Tears dripped along the crow's feet on my father's face.

I handed the letter to my father. He laid it on his chest and smoothed the paper with his hand. The message had been delivered. I felt a lot of satisfaction that Geraldo had been able to hear these tender words, and to know that he had made a difference in a young girl's life.

Yet, my mission did not feel accomplished. It felt more confused and complicated now than it had at the beginning. Why had he put my mother's address in the packet of gum? After all these years, was he hanging on to the idea he would return? Maybe he kept the address for more practical reasons. If he died in the desert, my mother, as an American, would be most equipped to deal with events in the United States. His other wife was dead. His son was a wanted man in Arizona. Nobody, I supposed, not even a tough old coyote, wanted a completely anonymous death.

Why he carried my mom's address was the least of my questions. Did my father want to stay here? Did he risk prosecution if he did? Since the man with him in the desert was dead, did any evidence exist for a human trafficking case? Did my father have anything to do with his death? This letter, I realized linked him to both. I eyed the paper spread across his hospital gown.

"I think I better keep that."

He nodded. I hastily folded the binder paper, stuck it back in the envelopes, and returned the worn pink package to my pocket.

Nurse Grace had mentioned members of the sheriff's department coming to the hospital. Did they still want to question my father?

My father dried both eyes with his right hand. Now did not seem the time to ask all these questions. I breathed in the hospital air, bitter and numbing as Novocain.

My eyes drifted to the red indentation on his head. Maybe if he stayed in the United States, he could be moved to one of those special facilities for the brain injured. Did they even have such a thing in Mexico? Was my father competent to make decisions about his future care?

I scooted the chair nearer his bed and sat, feeling paralyzed with indecision. I needed help.

I took my father's right hand. It was damp from his tears. "Papa?" It sounded so strange.

The tenderness in his eyes struck terror in my heart. I felt as though I were tumbling into a deep and unknown space that would reshape my skin, and transform my identity. When I pulled away from his gaze, I would be possessed, no longer Carol Sabala, but *hija*, daughter, precious, loved, treasure. I shut my eyes against the force of his love.

"Do you want to stay here or go back to Mexico?" I asked.

CHAPTER 35

Mexico.

"I am Mexican," he had said, tapping his heart. In the hospital, *Los Estados Unidos* had been fine, but at the prospect of leaving the facility, he was adamant that he return to Mexico.

Now I sat on my hotel bed wondering what to do. I couldn't consult his son. Geraldo, my half-brother, had apparently disappeared, worried about becoming bounty.

"Mark Escalante, you are a swine," I whispered aloud to the room.

Who, besides my half-brother, could give me advice? I could call David Shapiro and ask him if he wanted to take a trip to Mexico with me, but one of his complaints about our relationship had been that I turned to him only when I needed help.

I lay back on the neatly made bed and stared at the blank ceiling, counting the obstacles between here and Mexico. Would the hospital simply let my father go? Or would they hound me to claim him, to cough up a social security number, to sign up for his care? How did we travel to Mexico when he had no passport, no driver's license, no identification at all? We would have to drive, in spite of all the strictures and warnings at the Avis counter. On the positive side, if I took my rented car into Mexico, I obviously would not be the first person to do so. But where did my father go once we got to Mexico? His son had left Zihuatanejo, no doubt headed for Naco. If I took my father home, I'd have to make sure Mark Escalante didn't follow us right to his son.

I rolled over, reached for the phone and punched in the number of Sloan's Investigative Services, but as I listened to the ring, I knew J.J. Sloan would not be in the office. As the distorted sound of my own voice answered, I returned the phone to its cradle. This was not a Sloan's Investigative Services' case. He and I weren't chums. I respected him as an investigator, but otherwise regarded him as a pretentious, socially inept alcoholic who retained me only because he could no longer tolerate wife-in-hotel-with-boss cases.

I collapsed back on the bed. I missed the flitting geckos and clunking ceiling fan of Mexico. The nurse had said my father could walk. I thought of *The Purloined Letter*. In that Poe story, the best hiding spot for the letter had been out in the open, so obvious no one considered looking there. A scheme took shape for getting my father out of the hospital.

And the best help for taking him over the border was right in front of my eyes.

The next day, I did two things that were unusual for me; I measured and I shopped.

Even when I baked at Archibald's, I resisted measuring, so it was odd to buy a cloth tape and attempt to run it precisely from my dad's shoulder to wrist and from his waist to his ankle. I jotted down numbers and prattled.

"If they kept your clothes, they are probably blood-stained. Besides they obviously would not fit you anymore."

His eyes twinkled, amused.

We distracted ourselves from the embarrassing intimacy of the process by formulating a plan. This was ninety-nine percent me rambling and him adding an occasional word or a nod of the head.

I used the tape to assess more than his physical dimensions. With the lack of mobility in his left arm and hand, buttons were out. But he was able to hold the tape to his right shoulder, to lift his neck when I circled it, and to arch his back as I passed the tape under it.

"How far can you walk?"

"They take me up the hall," he said slowly, "until I'm tired." He paused as though formulating his next sentence. "But I could walk farther."

"What size shoe do you wear?"

I was not the kind of woman who liked to putter about Macy's, and shopping for someone else was even more brutal. I started at a Western wear store, figuring my father could manage snaps and that a Western shirt would suit an older Hispanic male. I entered the store completely unprepared for the battery of choices before me, regular or long, tapered or not, cotton, polyester, or blend. The store carried flashy satin rodeo shirts and blue chambray shirts that looked like they belonged on a San Quentin inmate. It took me an hour to decide on blue-checked cotton and the entire afternoon to complete his wardrobe, spending at least a half-hour at Sears walking back and forth between a shelf of boxers and a shelf of briefs.

I returned to the hospital in time to find him sitting up and eating dinner.

I pulled out the clothing items one by one. He smiled at the shirt. "Very nice." He nodded at the Levi's and black socks. He frowned at the briefs.

"I couldn't decide. These are what my former husband wore."

"It's okay." He picked up a green grape and chewed it slowly. His eyes switched over to the door.

"How are you doing this evening?" Nurse Grace pleasantly asked him.

"Good. Good," he replied.

I hastily stuffed the clothes in the shopping bag and turned around.

"I see you have company again," Nurse Grace said. "Is this reporter pestering you with questions?"

My father didn't respond.

"I'm a private investigator," I confessed. "I'm looking for a missing person." True enough.

"Okay," she said briskly.

I handed her my card from Sloan's Investigative Services. She glanced at it and stuck it in her pocket. "What are those clothes for?"

"The patient."

"Why?"

"To wear."

"And when exactly is he going to wear them?" She folded her arms over her uniform.

"When he gets out of the hospital."

"Is he your *missing person*?"

"Maybe."

She glowered.

"And since when do private investigators buy clothes for missing persons?"

"I'm not the usual kind of investigator."

"I'll say." She opened my father's straw, stuck it into his juice drink, and hinged it. This was the kind of work for an aide, not an RN.

"Do you work this shift tomorrow?" I asked.

"Yes I do," she said stiffly, "and the next night, too." Her voice was a warning. She stared at the open shoebox, as though noting every incriminating detail and then departed in her own due time.

I avoided my father's eyes. Our plan called for a late afternoon departure, so we could drive toward the border at an unsuspicious hour, but arrive as the sun was setting. If driving across proved problematic, Geraldo knew other ways into Mexico. However, our time frame meant we would have to walk out of the hospital during Nurse Grace's shift.

"We can watch her, too," my father said.

I glanced at him. His pale lips stretched into a hint of the razzle-dazzle smile I'd seen in the photos.

"*La Migra*'s mistake," he said, as he pushed aside the food tray. He lifted his body into a seated position. Bare white legs dangled from the bed. "They don't understand," he said slowly as he shoved off onto his feet, "we watch them, too."

The flat white feet showed off their bones. His ankles were as delicate and insubstantial as a colt's. In his hospital gown, my father topped me only because of the fuzz of his new hair.

This mission was doomed.

"Come on," my father commanded.

I glanced at the room's clock. As we trudged down the hall, his left arm dangled helplessly and the left leg dragged, but he slapped away my efforts to help him. He moved slowly and purposefully.

I had been prepared to persuade my father not to take the most direct route, south to Nogales, but I didn't need to. He suggested the route by which he had entered, the less traveled Highway 286. This was good. If Mark Escalante decided to tail us, the farther from Naco, the better.

My father frowned in concentration and his lips moved silently as he formulated his next question. Then he asked slowly, "Do you know anyone in Tucson?"

"No." I stopped. "Well, I know one person, but he wouldn't help us. Not willingly, anyway."

We reached the exit. My father tagged the door to show he had made it all the way to the end. He grinned at me and turned around with all the flourish he could muster.

We inched our way back to the room. The eternity had taken ten minutes.

I slogged my way through the next day. I called La Pizza again to share the good news of locating our father, but at the sound of my voice, Ana slammed down the receiver. I called my neighbor in Santa Cruz to ask her to continue feeding Lola for a few more days. The hotel's bills for my calls would be exorbitant. I needed a cell phone, but mobile phones scared me.

They addicted people like crack. My friends purchased them for "emergencies" and wound up unable to select a head of lettuce in Safeway without calling someone.

I made my last, most difficult call, packed my clothes, checked out of the hotel, and ventured into the community where I ate tacos that I was too nervous to taste. I passed time with another trip to the Western wear store. My father had requested a cowboy hat, insisting that he would pay for everything when he was home. Buying clothes for myself was painful; buying clothes for a near stranger was excruciating.

The sales clerk was a chubby Mexican girl of about sixteen with clipped-back long hair draped down her red and white plaid western shirt. She gestured to the vast array of hats and asked, "Wool, fur, felt, or straw?"

I gaped and the girl rattled off choices. One could buy genuine buffalo, beaver, chinchilla or sable fur. I shook my head. That all sounded too hot, and expensive, but as I followed her along the long display of straw hats, the selection was just as daunting: Raffia, Mexican palm, panama, seagrass, bandera. . . .

The sales girl smiled helpfully. "Does he ride horses?"

I shrugged.

She eyed me doubtfully. I didn't know such a detail about my own father?

"What color does he like?"

I wanted to punt her to the curb, but she smiled pleasantly, expectantly.

I selected a raffia hat of taupe, a code name for all colors mixed together for the indecisive soul.

As I charged the purchase, I wondered what my mom would think if she could see me spending her hard-earned savings on my dad. In spite of his insistence that he would reimburse me, I didn't plan to accept a penny from him.

The sales girl was very good, smiling and inquiring if I would like to purchase a hatbox.

I shook my head, relieved to answer a question. I asked for

directions to the nearest hardware store. Unlike the I'm-too-entitled-to-be-working-here guy at the gas station store, this teenager smartly rattled off directions.

Outside I drew in the invigorating air. The dry, crisp, sage tang cleared the sinuses. Tucson was growing on me.

The next chore was simpler. I followed the girl's directions a few blocks to a hardware store where I purchased the other items my father had requested: a sturdy pair of wire cutters and a roll of duct tape.

From there I headed back toward the airport, making a pit stop at a gas station to top off the tank. In the attached mini-store I purchased my father's last items: two liter-and-a-half bottles of water—a good supply, but still portable.

I hoped at the border my father and I would be waved through, that the authorities simply viewed prohibited rental cars as cash rolling into Mexico, and that they didn't bother checking the papers of passengers, but just in case everything was not smooth sailing, my father was devising a Plan B. He fretted that even though the Sheriff's Office lacked either the interest or the manpower to post someone at his hospital room, they might have asked the *Federales* to watch for him.

We'd had our first disagreement. He'd wanted a truck, but I'd balked at driving a huge vehicle. Since he didn't put up an argument, at the airport I exchanged the silver Prizm for a black one. At least he was getting his color.

"Do you have any maps of Arizona?" I asked the clerk.

"No, ma'am, but we have two of the broader Tucson area."

I took them both.

I sat in the Avis garage in my new car and studied the maps. Then I adjusted my seat and the mirrors and fiddled with all the dials even though the car model was exactly the same as my last one. I watched the clock crawl its way through the afternoon.

At 4:30, I pulled into the hospital parking lot. Like most institutions, the hospital served supper early and the start of feeding time created a flurry of activity. I strolled down the hall to the public restrooms, tossed the bag of clothing in the men's and then, as if noticing my error, backed out quickly and entered the women's. After a pause, I left the restroom and roamed the halls until Nurse Grace spotted me and followed me to Information.

When the first food carts hit the hallway, my father would begin a pre-prandial stroll.

At the desk, I asked the location of the other John Doe.

"What are you up to now?" Nurse Grace asked.

"I just thought I should check out this other guy," I said casually. "As a private investigator, I might stumble across someone who is looking for the guy with the broken leg."

I stalled, asking the information woman for a schedule of visiting hours, which I already had memorized.

She looked to Nurse Grace, who pointed impatiently at the posted times.

As I started for the room of John Doe *numero dos*, Nurse Grace dogged my heels. I walked at half my normal gallop.

"This is the wrong way," she said.

"Oh." I stopped and glanced around. "Do you want to escort me?"

She clearly would rather kiss a leper, but as I anticipated, she intended to keep an eye on me. She stood, arms akimbo, as I bent down to tie my shoe. Did she suspect what we were up to and secretly support our effort?

I peeked up to see Mark Escalante strolling down the hall with all his cocky, clean-cut bravado packed into jeans, a black tee-shirt, and his Arizona chic of boots and hat. No doubt about it, he was a good-looking prick.

Nurse Grace appraised him. Mark must have known his initial impact all too well. I remembered my first impression—the muscles, the age appropriateness, the lack of wedding band, and the subtle cologne.

"So where is this guy?" Mark asked brusquely.

Nurse Grace looked from Mark to me and back.

In my normal life in Santa Cruz, I worked for an officious, verbose kitchen manager named Eldon. I channeled him now and introduced Nurse Grace and Mark, explaining to Nurse Grace that Mark was a bounty hunter that I had met in Zihuatanejo while I was vacationing, blah, blah, blah. When Mark's eyes began to bulge, I wrapped up quickly with, "This man can take the young John Doe off your hands."

Nurse Grace heaved a sigh. "So this little number about being a private investigator who might find someone to help this guy was just another of your lies."

I shrugged and left her to her inner debate. She hesitated, caught in the thrall of Mark, but torn between freeing a bed and sending a young patient to jail.

I excused myself to use the restroom. Mark's eyes burned into my skull, but I didn't turn. When I had called him from the hotel in the morning, he had been downright nasty and distrusting on the phone. "Why would you want to help me?"

"So you forget about Geraldo Sabala in Mexico."

He'd barked a cruel laugh. "You're proposing a trade. What if your guy isn't worth as much as Geraldo?"

"There's a huge convenience factor here for you."

"How do you know there's a reward for this guy?"

"My father fingered him."

"You better not be fucking with me, Carol."

I gulped. My mom always said my face was an "open book." I was glad that we were on the phone and Mark couldn't see me. "You better not fuck with me either. If you collar this John Doe, you better not come after Geraldo."

"Or what, Carol?" He sounded mightily superior. "You'll slap me again?" He hung up.

As Nurse Grace guided Mark toward the mute, unsuspecting, and most likely worthless John Doe, I laughed inside all the way to the door of the men's restroom. Revenge was sweet. Even if the plan had flaws, like rekindling Mark's wrath,

I loved the beauty of it. Keeping the nurse and Mark occupied with each other killed two birds with one stone, as my mom would say. I pulled the bathroom door and it gave way. I stumbled backward.

"Wrong door, lady," said a black male nurse.

As my heartbeat stilled, I allowed myself a glance up the hall, but Nurse Grace and Mark had turned into the corridor for John Doe's room.

The nurse towered above me. Not just tall, but big, like a football tackle. "Are you all right?"

"Fine. The patient in 142 was having some trouble though. He was choking on his food."

He looked alarmed. "Did you inform anyone?"

"I'm informing you."

I could tell he wanted to ask me a few questions, like why I was looking for help in the men's room, but he hustled away.

My father emerged, transformed and handsome. The big cowboy hat covered the ugly scar and shadowed his hospital pallor. The crisp shirt accented his broad shoulders and the lack of the paunch he'd had in the photographs. We exited the hospital and walked carefully to the black Prizm illegally parked in the loading zone.

I peeled out, my heart racing with the sense of adventure, The Big Get-Away.

"Careful," my father admonished.

Our street to the freeway was called Speedway, but I slowed down and obeyed all the traffic lights. My father was right. We didn't want to be stopped now.

Would Nurse Grace bother to call the cops? What would she say? That a patient walked out? Since in her own assessment "he could probably survive on his own," how excited would the police be? Grace couldn't report him as an illegal immigrant, because as far as she knew, he was a legal resident, perhaps even a citizen, married to my mother. Of course, there was the matter of the dead guy in the desert with a slug in his back. Did the nurse know about that? I glanced at my father. He gazed out his window, a serene expression on his face.

Maybe the nurse would sigh and be happy to have an open hospital bed. Two, if the other John Doe turned out to be someone Mark could use.

If the John Doe was worthless, Mark would be pissed. I wished I could see his face.

I smiled and patted the steering wheel of my new rental as I veered onto Ajo Way. On the map, I had thought the dot for Three Points took its name from the T intersection of Highway 86 and Highway 286, but now our car pointed toward three peaks, etched against the blue sky the way a child would draw mountains.

The traffic thinned as we headed into the stunted trees and cacti. City noise gave way to a silence that permeated the car. A border patrol truck, white with green lettering, passed us, an all-terrain vehicle in its bed. My heart thudded, but the officer zoomed by without a second look. I tried to reassure myself that we weren't doing anything terribly wrong, just skipping out on a monumental bill that the hospital didn't expect to collect anyway. Just taking a rented car across the border like a billion other non-rule-abiding tourists. Just praying no one at the border crossing would demand my father's I.D. Just removing an eyewitness to a murder.

I peeked in the rearview mirror and then back to the straight line of highway.

My father observed the brush, a slight smile on his face. He zipped open a window and drew a deep breath of air. The day was still and surprisingly warm. When he closed the window, quiet enveloped us.

Dwarfed in the expanse of open space, the telephone poles tipped precariously in the sand. Civilization melted away to sandy, bare stretches of sagebrush. My eyes darted to this stranger beside me. This foreigner. This alien.

"I met your son in Mexico," I launched in Spanish.

He smiled. "You speak good Spanish."

"And Ana and your granddaughter." Any real conversation would be difficult for him, but the silence spooked me.

Another border patrol vehicle swished by, heading toward Tucson.

This territory was crawling with them. What an odd job, to try to eliminate your *raison d'etat.*

The officer's head did not swivel. He had zero interest in a rented black Prizm with a female driver that wasn't coming from Mexico. But I couldn't shake the sense of dislocation and nervousness that came from being in this strange terrain, the sweeping vistas across sand and desolation. I had no idea if the John Doe in the hospital was worth anything to Mark or not, but if not, how long would it take him to discover he had been duped?

My guess—not long. His intelligence had been part of what attracted me.

I regretted having chosen Spanish for conversation with my father, since I could not babble in it. I had to concentrate and search for words as I told him about my trip to Zihuatanejo.

I avoided the question I wanted to ask: What about the dead guy you were with?

Three Points was a place ready to vanish from future maps. On the far side of the intersection stood a restaurant and a small adobe church without a single car in the worn asphalt lot. The near side featured a gas station and liquor store combo lined with several cars, including a white and green Immigration and Naturalization SUV. I turned south on 286 and headed toward the border.

"You are not married?" my passenger asked, voice soft, eyes averted.

"No."

"Children?" His tone was tragic.

"Nope." I glanced toward him and then followed his gaze out to an arroyo cut in the sand.

"Very dangerous," he said, tapping on the window. "People hide and then the water rushes down." He swooshed his good hand to illustrate. Life could be over in an instant. And no children, no legacy, the sadness of that idea traveled from his bent neck down to his boots.

If I told him I didn't want any rug rats, would he think I belonged in a freak show? I couldn't muster the exact vocabulary to voice my thoughts in Spanish, so I said in English, "Some people are not meant to be parents."

His head whipped around. His expression shattered like baked marbles. The left eye drooped with tragic sadness.

"I didn't mean you," I said quickly in English. But maybe I did. Part of me wondered why I was helping this guy. What had he done for me in the last forty-two years? Why hadn't he loved us like he did his new family?

He didn't even share my nervousness when an INS van rolled toward us.

"*M'ija*, I am sorry," he said solemnly in Spanish. The new duds no longer hid his pallor, and he sank into the seat.

As he passed us, the INS officer raised a finger from his steering wheel in greeting. I gripped the wheel and raised my eyes to the rearview, waiting for the van to disappear, but the road was flat and straight and the van was in no hurry. My eyes blurred. I pulled to the side of the road. I swiped at my eyes. "Get out."

"*M'ija*," he implored.

"It's not that," I snapped. "The van stopped." Fighting tears, I unclipped my seatbelt, twisted in my seat, my rib screaming in protest, and dug through my suitcase. I stuck my unused instamatic into his startled hand. I slammed out of the car and stalked to the side of the road. Surprisingly balmy air caressed my face. The sun was low in the sky, providing just enough light to make my ruse credible.

Geraldo awkwardly climbed from his side and pushed the door shut with his right hip. He shuffled a few steps. The redolence of creosote hung in the air as though it had recently rained.

The van doubled back. I didn't want the officer even to inquire casually if we were on our way to Mexico.

"Take pictures of me with that in the background." I pointed at a distant lone flat-topped peak that jutted into the sky like Devil's Tower. I stretched my lips into an imitation of a smile.

He pushed the button. In the opposite lane, the van slowed.

"Take another one," I shouted brightly.

The camera and hand covered his face.

"Wait," I said. I pushed wiry hairs off my cheek. "Cheeeesssse."

The white van slowed to a near stop. The driver leaned our way, examining us.

"Shii-eeet," I murmured for my next smile. Had I made everything worse by stopping? Should I wave at the officer?

At least my plan created a reason for my father to keep his back to the man.

The guy seemed about to stop, but then continued by. I watched him leave up the lonely road. From the other direction, a black car, shimmering in the sun, crested a dusty knoll. While I had been driving prissily at the speed limit, the Charger was traveling so fast it looked as though it could launch into the air.

"Get in the car. Quick."

I pulled Geraldo toward our vehicle and pushed him roughly into the seat. He lifted the helpless left leg in and then swung in the right. Mark Escalante had reached us and skidded to a stop, sending up a plume of dust. I raced to the driver's side, fell into my seat, and pulled the door, but Mark Escalante caught the handle. We competed in a panting tug of war. My father leaned over my body with his good arm, caught the side pocket of the door and yanked.

Mark Escalante dug in and used his body weight.

"What do you want?" I yelled.

"You know what I want."

"No I don't."

"What you owe me!" he shouted.

"I don't owe you shit." My shoulders were going to pull out of their sockets.

Mark snarled at me. "Geraldo Sabala or something better. A deal is a deal."

My father gasped. "He wants me?" He released his hold on the door.

Where the hell was the INS when you needed them?

I let go of my hold, too. The door flew open and Mark Escalante tumbled to the ground.

I cranked the key and hit the gas. Mark Escalante was smart enough to let go of the handle.

I slowed enough to shut the door. "He doesn't want you," I explained to my father. "I wasn't going to sell you out. He wants your son. For the reward money."

I drove the speed limit. There wasn't any escape. We were on a straight, isolated road to the Mexican border. Soon enough the black Charger loomed behind us. I had to give the man credit for deducing our destination and route. Or, more likely, making a lucky guess.

"Why is he chasing you?"

"Your son has disappeared from Zihuatanejo, and that guy thinks I know where Geraldo is."

"Naco?"

Taking in his cowboy hat, I replied, "I reckon."

"Then I can't go home," he said matter of factly.

FUBAR. The handy word surfaced from my teens: Fucked up beyond all repair. "Maybe it's time to visit your granddaughter."

He was silent. Once in Mexico, maybe we could travel to the nearest airport and get him on a plane toward Zihua. I savored the idea of Mark Escalante hitting a dead end, of watching my father travel to the one place Mark knew did not harbor his prey. But even that would require some ID.

"I have money," I volunteered.

He didn't speak.

I glanced nervously in the rearview, but the black metal of Mark's car was disappearing into darkness. Stark, empty desert spread on both sides of the highway. I tried to imagine people out there, threading their way through the cacti and shrubs, hiding in the arroyos, baking in the sun, freezing at night, risking death from dehydration and flash floods. At the moment I could not imagine how something like my life in America could possibly be worth the risk they were taking.

We rode for a while in silence, my stomach flipping like a landed fish, my palms sweating on the steering wheel. After several minutes, my father commanded, "Turn here."

"The gate's closed," I argued. But I made the turn onto a bumpy, dirt road. What difference did it make? We weren't going to lose Mark Escalante. And now that the car doors were locked, what could he do except berate me?

I kept the car engine running although we weren't exactly going anywhere with a barbed-wire gate in front of us. Mark Escalante stopped behind us, and leaving his lights shining into the descending dark, stomped toward our car. After I had slapped him, he had threatened to kill me. I had just dumped his keister in the dirt. I doubted he took kindly to that.

CHAPTER 36

Mark Escalante smiled and rapped on the glass. He mimed rolling down a window.

I shook my head.

A passing INS truck slowed down to take a good look at us. Mark Escalante tipped his hat at him, and the truck rolled on.

"Open the fucking window, Carol," Mark growled.

"Or what?"

In his line of work, I was sure Mark, like myself, had a permit to carry, but no firearm could be hidden in his tight clothing. I lifted in my seat and tried to peer down to his boots.

But Mark had no need for a gun. He gestured at the desert and laughed. Behind me the Charger blocked our exit and spotlighted the scene in the gathering gloom. On the ranch land, about thirty feet in front of us, a tall saguaro cactus raised its arms as though in surrender.

My father unlocked his door and swung it open.

"What are you doing?"

As he used his good arm to lift his damaged leg out the door, I caught his shirt collar and yanked him back.

Mark Escalante circled the car. He grabbed my father by one leg and a belt loop. "Want to get out?" he said, jerking Geraldo to his feet.

I released the collar so as not to strangle my father.

Mark pushed Geraldo forward and my father fell into the sand. Then in one fluid movement, before I could even think to bolt, Mark plopped into the passenger seat and latched on to my arm. "Alone at last."

My heart pounded. My father pushed himself onto all fours, struggled up, and brushed off his pants. Even with his naturally thick chest and with clothes that fit, he looked insubstantial.

Mark watched him plant his hat back over his pale, haggard face.

"Let's talk business."

I kept my eyes on my father. Unperturbed, he limped toward the gate and grappled with it. What the hell was he doing? Fleeing? I felt angry. Mark was so cocky, he hadn't even locked the door. Why wasn't my father attacking him, trying to help me?

"Head injury," Mark smirked. "No water. Even in the winter, he won't last long, and then he'll be just another dead Mexican in the desert." He made no move to turn off my car engine. He turned on the air-conditioner, which squealed to life. The evening wasn't particularly warm, but a patina of sweat glistened on his forehead. My arms pocked with bumps as he sat in cool comfort and watched my father work a loop of wire up a post.

"You're of Mexican descent, aren't you?" I charged.

"I'm American."

"You speak Spanish."

"I celebrate the Fourth of July, not *Cinco de Mayo*."

"Mexican Independence Day is September sixteenth."

"Right there's my point."

"That's just ignorance."

"Carol, you just do not know when to shut up." He squeezed my cold arm, pinching the skin between his fingers, sure to leave bruises like on a choke victim. His body pressed so close I could feel its heat. And its power. As much as I wanted to rake my fingernails, nubby as they were, across his eyeballs, my body shrank back against the car door.

"I don't know where Geraldo Sabala is."

"You are not a good liar, Carol." His sweat and cologne dominated the car's interior.

"So my mom always told me." The goose bumps rippled up my arms to my neck and skull. At least I wouldn't be humiliated by a hot flash.

Limping, my father slowly dragged the gate open. The motion he made was subtle, but unmistakable. I grabbed the steering wheel with my free hand and stepped on the gas. We lurched forward, and Mark let go of my arm so I could steer and he could brace himself.

We bumped over a cattle guard. The dirt road veered sharply to the left to avoid the saguaro cactus. We bounced a short distance before Mark reached over and switched off the ignition. We rocked to a stop.

"That was stupid," he said.

I had to agree. I looked around in amazement. Behind us, lit up by Mark's headlights, my father was closing the gate, conscientious even in a crisis, even when every movement was an effort, even when no cattle were visible and their existence seemed doubtful. Since my body had no escape, my mind decided to run. What did the cows eat? Mesquite? They damn sure didn't nibble the barrel cactus.

Why didn't my father stay on the other side of the fence, take Mark's car and come roaring after us?

"I thought of something."

He snorted. "About time."

Had I not noticed his coldness in Zihuatanejo? My first impression had been of confidence, power and privilege. I had been attracted. What did that say about me? On the other hand, what would it say if I were attracted to weak, wimpy men? Could a woman find a confident, powerful man who wasn't a bit of an ass?

I glanced in the rearview. My father trudged up the road, pulling his weak left leg behind him. The sun had worked its way behind the mountaintops. This was January. When the sun dropped below the horizon, it would be dark. The temperature would plummet.

"I can give you someone else."

He barked a laugh. "Like the John Doe in the hospital?"

"No," I said calmly. In the mirror I watched my father bend down. I reached for the door handle, but Mark clutched a bundle of my thick hair and snapped my head back.

"Don't even think about it."

"No wonder you like this type of hair."

He tightened his grip, arching my neck. His breath prickled my skin.

"My father collapsed," I rasped.

He glanced in the side mirror and shook his head. "Nice try, Nancy Drew." He used my hair to launch me forward. My sternum cracked into the steering wheel, sending pain like sparks through my chest. I coughed, which hurt even more.

Nancy Drew. I wanted to kill him. Only David got to call me Nancy Drew.

I straightened and noticed through blurry eyes that my father was up and slowly, inexorably drawing nearer. I clearly had not inherited stubbornness only from my mom.

As the sun fell, the mountains turned into silhouettes. "Do you remember the guy in Zihuatanejo who tried to drown me?"

Mark poked off the air conditioning and smiled like the thought of my drowning appealed to him. "Go on."

"Did you ever wonder why he went after me?" I forced myself not to check on my father. I couldn't see now, anyway. I believed in the figure approaching through the gathering darkness, in the man Mark regarded as a piece of garbage.

Mark's eyes narrowed. "Believe it or not, Carol, I was focused on a few other things in Zihua besides you—like Lalo de la Cruz and your buddy, brother, wanted criminal Geraldo Sabala."

"That guy who attacked me ran with Lalo de la Cruz , but I think you figured that out."

"Yeah, well, thanks to you, I never got a scope on him, and I don't know his name. He's worthless to me."

"I know his name."

He shrugged, but leaned back, the body language moving from intimidation to negotiation. "That still doesn't mean he's worth anything."

"He went back to Zihua at the same time Lalo did."

Mark thought about the implications. Did any of his actions have to do with vigilante justice, or did all his pursuits end at the bottom line? While I was often motivated by the former, my boss J.J. Sloan kept reminding me, as a business, we had to worry about the latter. I felt my attitude toward Mark soften one degree. He'd chosen an occupation where a person couldn't afford to be Mr. Nice Guy. "Keep it business," I coached myself. I hoped that the victim's family had extended the reward to cover all parties involved in the murder—that it increased with each guilty rat.

"I'll give you the name if you give up on Geraldo Sabala."

"How do I know you won't make up the name?"

"As you yourself mentioned, I'm a terrible liar. Secondly, the guy who tried to kill me is a slimy piece of shit. Why wouldn't I give him up? Finally, how do I know you will stop searching for Geraldo?"

He heaved a sigh. "Ah, yes, trust." He clasped his hands, steepled two fingers, and tapped them on his lips. He didn't seem the least bit concerned that this left him open to a quick punch in the gut.

We were at an impasse, which was fine with me. The longer he waited, the closer my father came.

He released his hands. We sat silently in the dark on a deserted road. The Mark Escalante I had met en route to Zihuatanejo reinhabited the form beside me, and I realized the man in the car with me had always been there, too. I just had not seen him, or hadn't wanted to see him. But I had known he was a bounty hunter almost from the start, a profession that demanded a person be determined and cold.

"Okay," he said impatiently. "Shoot."

"Hugo."

"That's it," he said angrily. "Just a first name?"

"Promise me you will drop the search for Geraldo."

"What is this, grade school? Do you want to prick fingers and rub our blood together?"

"No. My brother died from AIDS." After all these years, I was amazed how Donald could spring up, anywhere, anytime, like an unpredictable Jack-in-the-Heart.

Mark Escalante fell silent. Perhaps even he could be chagrined.

I risked a peek in the mirror. Black silence had swallowed my father. Headlights arced over the sand. They turned about a half mile back, where Mark's car sat deserted by the road, shining into the desert. "We have company."

Mark swiveled in his seat. "*La Migra*. Let's wrap this up."

I debated my options. They had spotted Mark's deserted car. How long before they opened the gate and started up the road? Would they search the car and run the plates first?

While the officers might neutralize any threat from Mark, what did they mean for my father? What would they make of an old Mexican man hobbling up a desert road? A Mexican man with no proper identification?

"His last name was Morales. Hugo Morales."

Click.

Mark swung. The passenger door flew open and a rock came down on his head. He yelped in surprise and threw his arms up to cover himself.

My father brought down the rock on Mark's elbow. Mark leaned back and cocked his leg, but before he could kick, I grabbed his family jewels and squeezed like I meant to make juice. It took the thrust out of his thrust.

"Ooof." The sound didn't need any translation. Mark's kick had connected.

Mark dropped his arms and elbowed back into my gut. The blow to my solar plexus paralyzed me. I let go of his balls. I couldn't breathe or move. My heart felt like it had stopped. I tested my ability to move my fingers and wrapped them limply around the tail of Mark's shirt that had pulled loose from his jeans.

Through my haze I heard a crack and Mark cried out again.

"Get out," my father hissed. "Or I will kill you."

"Stop!" I heard myself say. "This is crazy."

As Mark Escalante lifted himself from the bucket seat, I released my handful of fabric. He collapsed onto the sand. If things had been complicated before, how would I explain the crumpled body of Mark Escalante to the Border Patrol?

"What are you doing?" I cried.

Being a good dad. Protecting his kids.

Shushing me, my father fell into the seat, loaded his leg, and locked the door. Sound traveled in the clear desert air, the officers' ears probably already pricked, alert, their heads turning our way.

I massaged my aching chest. "They will find him," I said. "He will tell them everything."

"Start the car," he ordered, panting. "No lights. Drive slow and straight." He held his side. What a pathetic duo we were. He had lost his hat in the struggle and the paleness of his head glowed eerily.

I did as told because I didn't have any other plan. Even though Mark had turned off the air-conditioner, the engine still sounded like a roar. Good thing I didn't have a truck.

My trembling hands gripped the steering wheel. "This is all fine for you," I said angrily in English. "You're going to Mexico. I'm staying here in the States, and that guy back there knows who I am. We just assaulted him. How is that protecting me?"

He looked away and didn't answer.

I seethed. Maybe this was only about protecting his son. His real family. He needed to get rid of Mark so he could return to Naco. Go back to Geraldo.

Behind us lights bounced, aimed westward, then stopped.

Closing the gate like good citizens. As they turned toward us our road dipped and their lights disappeared. My stomach rose as though with the sudden drop of an elevator. The sky now was black. No moon had risen yet. I drove blindly along at ten miles per hour.

"Turn at the prickly pear."

I couldn't see any cactus, and didn't know how he could either unless he had the eyes of a nocturnal creature. Or unless he knew the area so well he didn't even need eyes. I assumed, though, that he meant toward the right since to the left would take us back toward the fence.

The car didn't bottom out in sand so I figured I'd managed to stay on a ranch road, but I suddenly wished I had opted for a truck. The scene became lighter, like someone had flicked on a grand nightlight. Outlines of brush emerged from the darkness, and I accelerated to twenty miles per hour.

"Turn here." He spoke like an omniscient swami.

I could dimly see that a fork in the road led to the left. I steered up a slight incline. The Prizm started to vibrate. Behind us light played over the desert, illuminating mesquite and washes in the sand. The light splayed from a fixed point well behind us. They must have reached Mark Escalante.

Our car felt as though it was tipping, and the steering wheel cranked to the side. "I think we have a flat tire."

Up in front of us, at a distance, dogs barked. They did not sound friendly.

"Stop here," my father said, as though I had much choice. He pointed at a turnout behind a bush of mesquite.

I pulled the shuttering car in.

"Follow me."

During the next few weeks, I had many opportunities to wonder why I obeyed my father. My instincts told me to walk back and try to reason with the Border Patrol officers, not to get out of the car and to trudge over the desert like an illegal immigrant, with an old crippled man, no less. He handed me one of the bottles of water. He carried his bottle in a plastic bag with the wire cutters and duct tape.

Maybe I wanted to please my father. Maybe I wanted him to acknowledge that I was as valuable as his son. I knew the whole thing was insane at the time, but I didn't see any good way out.

"I know this area," he whispered.

The racket of the dogs pierced the desert air. We moved in the direction of the noise, where a bright, blazing yard light replaced dim house lights.

My father slid into a wash and I tumbled after. We sat at the bottom of the draw in the warm sandy soil. In the distance, the dogs yammered and bounced against chain link fence. The truck approached. My father labored for breath. It was a miracle he had made it this far. I'd come searching for my inheritance, and part of the gold was willpower. As a child I had imagined that I would be the next Yuri Geller, able to bend spoons with the force of my will. I had even practiced, trying to make my brother's nose hook down. In spite of all empirical evidence to the contrary, belief in my own supernatural power and indestructibility remained. My mom had been a completely practical soul. Clearly this trait came from my father.

I wonder what passed through his head. Did he realize then that he was an old man with a brain injury, that he was no longer capable of walking miles through the desert? And even if he could, would it only be to lead Mark Escalante to his son?

The vehicle came, slowed, and continued past the turn where I'd stashed the Prizm.

"Stay here." My father pointed at a fissure in the bank with an overhanging clump of brush.

"While you do what?"

"Look for transportation."

I didn't want him to leave me alone in the dark.

"They won't see you even with lights. Even with *helicóptero.*" He lightly, quickly, tentatively touched my face and brushed away hair. "*M'ija*."

My heart melted, and I backed into the crack, not even wide enough to spread my arms.

He dragged himself along the draw. I listened to his slow progress. The dogs calmed to growls and suspicious whines. I imagined them pacing the fence, sniffing. I heard the engine again, growing louder, returning, coming back to where the road forked.

The little cave was cool and smelled of earth. I stood rigidly, arms wrapped around myself, thinking of spiders, rattlesnakes, and scorpions. Blood pulsed in my neck and fingertips. My heart beat in my ears and feet. If my father found transportation, a vehicle, a horse, a bicycle, did he plan to come back for me? Why would he? My final destination was not Mexico. He never came back before.

I felt sad, the sadness of being left in a dark hole. Deserted.

The vehicle pursuing us sounded big and powerful. It slowed and made the turn. At the house up ahead, the dogs renewed their barking. The truck stopped. Doors slammed. They had reached my rental car. Footsteps. Voices. More car doors, looking inside. Flickers and flashes of light.

I could no longer hear my father.

So what if they didn't spot me? What was I supposed to do? Hang out in a desert hole until they left? Then what? Change the flat on my rental car and simply go on my merry way? As though they wouldn't be able to check on it, find out my name, question me later?

The light swept down into the gully. I raised my hands and stepped out of the crevice so that they could see me.

Even though I identified myself and stated that I was an American citizen, one officer trained a gun on me while the other slid into the wash and patted me down. He was an older man who looked Hispanic. He pushed me up the sandy bank while the other officer reached down to clasp my hand and hoist me. I landed helplessly on the rim of the wash like a hooked fish. Then the officer stooped down for his flashlight and blinded me far longer than necessary.

"Let me show you my driver's license." I couldn't see much but starry light and vague forms, but I imagined the gun in the officer's other hand.

As the second man scrabbled out of the gulley, I dusted myself off, stood slowly, and presented my driver's license to the officer who had hoisted me.

He tipped the flashlight toward my driver's license. "Where's your passenger?"

After a couple of eye squeezes, I could make out that he was a young, stringy Anglo. He holstered his gun.

"He's my father," I said. "He was married to my mother, an American citizen."

"Where is he?" He handed back my license and put the light in my face.

"I don't know."

We marched toward their SUV, which shone whitely in the beam of the flashlight. It was one of those large models with three rows of seats and no doubt four-wheel drive, good for the terrain and for hauling hordes of lawbreakers.

They had brought Mark with them, and his face grim, he leaned against their vehicle. They must have ordered him to stay back.

"Can you two kids behave in the backseat together?" the older officer asked.

My tall young escort directed me toward the opposite side of the SUV. Mark Escalante glared. A nice smear of blood covered his forearm.

The dogs yapped excitedly and everybody turned his gaze toward the lit-up yard of a distant ranch house.

Then a sonic crack cut through the night.

Mark and I sprang into the back seat, and the officers jumped into the front. The younger man punched the accelerator and drove toward the light while his partner called for backup. "Shot fired."

My head sprang toward the roof. My heart sank to the floor.

The truck's lights revealed scenery like an amateur film-maker, the images of pocked dirt road and desert brush jumping and jarring.

Mark used the occasion to lean across the seat and whisper hotly in my ear, "If Hugo isn't my reward for this shit, I'll not only get your brother, I'll be seeing you, too."

In hell, I thought, but my heart beat so fast and my lips were so dry, I couldn't utter a word.

CHAPTER 37

Guy Smith looked as one might picture an Arizona rancher--tall and leathery, decked out in jeans, boots and cowboy hat. Given to belt buckles and string ties. As much as I hated him, as much as I glared at him when he was sentenced, I could not escape my father's part in his own death. He had acted like someone committing suicide by rancher. My father knew the man hated illegals. That was part of the man's defense—the constant destruction to his ranch. The aliens littered, left piles of human excrement, stole his grandkids' bikes, bathed in his cows' troughs, cut his fences, and killed his dogs. Most people in the region felt sympathetic to his plight. Before the sentencing, he had been out of jail on his own recognizance.

My father knew Guy Smith would be armed. What rancher wasn't? In fact, he owned a .223 caliber Ruger Mini-14 "for coyote and prairie dog control." He carried it that night, an old rifle with rust pits in the steel barrel and dings on the stock from throwing it into the back of his pickup.

"I wish I'd a put a scope on it," he said in his deposition, "but the iron sights don't get beat up in the truck."

The prosecution jumped on this remark as evidence the rancher wanted to take aim at my father, but it didn't ring true.

What rang true was that the .22 caliber bullet left a small entry wound in my dad's chest, so when I bent over him that night, near the outer reaches of the rancher's bright yard light, I could see no reason for my father to be dead. What rang true were details: the gritty soil under my knees, the stiff and slick newness of my father's shirt, the sparkle of the snaps, the little hole, the dead weight of his body, the young officer's grasp on my shoulder, his fingers against my father's neck as he checked for a pulse.

"It was an accident." Those were the rancher's first words. He had been aiming to scare, not to kill. His dog had knocked into him.

Add good lawyers and Mark's willingness to swear that my father was dangerous, and Guy Smith faced only an involuntary manslaughter charge.

But the clincher was that this man had once saved my father's life, scaring off some drug dealers and calling for help. Guy Smith's deposition explained to me who had shot the young man with my father. With Guy Smith as a live, lucid witness to events, it was no wonder the sheriff's office had left my father unguarded in the hospital. They did not need his testimony regarding the murder, and they hardly had time to waste on just another immigrant.

How could I fault my father for returning to this ranch? The man had once saved his life. He probably would not have considered the rancher capable of murder, and this was a route he knew so well he could find his way in the dark.

So many events conspired to lead to that moment. If it weren't for a little girl's effort to say thank you to my father, if it weren't for that pink envelope, I might not have ever found Geraldo Sabala. I might have gone to my own grave with the scanty story of him that I had been fed. He never would have touched my face and called me *M'ija*.

But then, he might not have died.

I could not blame my father for limping toward that sandy yard only to receive a bullet in his chest. I could not blame him any more than I could regret traveling hundreds of miles to deliver a thank-you note. We all walked toward our end. In the meantime, the world needed more *gracias*.

"There's a silver lining in every cloud," my mother used to say. I've never been much of a silver lining person myself, but

I suppose there was one. I found myself sad to leave Tucson, but happy to be going home to Santa Cruz. David Shapiro had missed me. He had also done some legwork of his own.

As Lola wrapped herself around my ankle and meowed for more scratches under her chin, I listened to my phone messages. Wedged between hang-ups, a reminder that Lola was past due for her annual vet appointment, and a sweet message from my cousin Brandon saying he really hoped he ended up at UCSC, David had left five messages:

1. When are you coming home? I have exciting news. Call me.

2. Don't you retrieve your messages? Call me.

3. I found the perfect house for us. Call me.

4. What good is an answering machine if you don't check it? Call me when you get this.

5. We have to look at this house now. Call me.

No mushy "I love you," but "perfect house for us" said it all.

###

If you enjoyed *Death with Dessert*, please tell a friend about the book or consider writing a review. For more information, visit www.vinniehansen.com.

ACKNOWLEDGMENTS

I would like to thank Sue at Humane Borders for providing information about deaths in the desert. ZihuaRob of Zihuatanejo, Guerrero, México, and Alejandro of the Mexican Consulate in Tucson, Arizona, both deserve medals for their patience in answering my questions. Carin Hanna and author Lee Harris provided Tucson tidbits to fill in gaps from my visit. Members of my writing group, Brian Dutro, Edie Fischer, A. Fontenol, Pat Ihrig, Jack Jones, Bryn Kanar, James Moran, Rick Parfitt, Irene Reti, and Rona Yohalem, as well as my husband, Daniel S. Friedman, read and commented on the first draft of this book. My brother-in-law Al Vogan is my invaluable source of gun information, and Holly Bennett, RN and author, helped me with medical facts. Last, but not least, a big gracias to the ladies at misterio press.

RECIPE

If you've gone to a Mexican restaurant or traveled to Mexico, you've probably noticed the absence of abundant desserts. Mexican culture does not emphasize baked goods like pies and cakes, possibly because of the tropical heat or because wheat is not the commonly used grain. Most of the desserts that do exist are made on the stovetop rather than baked. Even the classic flan was traditionally cooked on the stovetop.

If you've ever ordered flan in a Mexican restaurant in the States, chances are you've received a delicious, light, custard-like dish with a bit of caramel syrup on top. The flan the Mexican-American parents of my students make, and the flan I've received in restaurants in Mexico are a similar, but heftier and more substantial, dessert. Put it this way, the flan I consider "real" Mexican flan can be cut and served like a cake.

Sylvia's Flan

8 oz. cream cheese at room temperature
5 eggs
1 8 oz. can of sweetened condensed milk
1 12 oz. can of evaporated milk
1 tsp. of vanilla (I use more!)

2 cups of sugar to make syrup (Or less. See directions.)

Directions: Heat oven to 350°F. Blend all of the ingredients except the sugar. (In spite of a ton of whisking on my part, the mixture was never 100% smooth.) Prepare the syrup by melting the sugar slowly in a saucepan over low heat, stirring constantly. (In my opinion, this creates more syrup than necessary. One could halve the amount.) Once the sugar has melted, pour the resulting syrup into an 8-inch square pan. (Organic sugar takes longer to melt, but creates a dark, non-traditional, smoky, almost molasses-like, syrup.) Let the syrup harden for 10 minutes. Pour the mixture of the other ingredients over the syrup. Place the 8-inch pan in a larger pan. Fill the larger pan with hot water to a half inch from the smaller pan's top. Bake for about an hour. To test the doneness of the flan, insert a knife into its center. The blade should pull out clean. Chill. Unmold at serving time by inverting the pan.